JULIE BALDWIN

A Very Okay Love Story

OTLCREATIVESTUDIOS

First edition

ISBN: 979-8-9898906-1-3

Editing by Betty Katowicius

This book was professionally typeset on Reedsy.
Find out more at reedsy.com

Dedicated
To Betty, for the help.
To Markus, for the love.
To my family, for the start.
To my kids, for the drive.
To anyone who has ever reinvented themselves, for the win.

Contents

1

Sherman Oaks Adjacent

When I was twenty-four, I was dating a guy who was so exciting . . . at first. He ticked off all these immediate boxes: attractive—check, charming—check, interesting and interested—check and check. Two months into our relationship, the signs were there. This was not the guy for me, but I held fast to that first impression. I held on to that initial potential. We dated far past our expiration date.

A few days after we finally broke it off, a friend brought over some wine and this beautiful, broken-in, red leather jacket she bought from a secondhand store on Lankershim Blvd.

Someone once loved this jacket. Felt like a million bucks in this jacket. Felt powerful and sexy. I wondered what changed that. What caused the former owner to let go of something that once made her feel good? How long did she keep the jacket hanging in her closet before she sent it on to a new life with a new owner?

Relationships are like clothes. They fit well at first. They make us feel good at the start. It's easy to hang on so tightly to that initial feeling, we don't notice when the relationship doesn't suit us anymore.

Excerpt from *Great Expectations* by April Townsend

So that was this. That fear of failure always hanging on her like a purse threatening to fall off her sloped shoulders, this is the place it lands—the signature line of divorce papers.

He could have asked for half her book earnings; after all, the story is half his. But he didn't. He asked for half the sale of the house and already made a down payment on an RV.

"That's funny, isn't it?" April laughs in that numb way one does when talking to their therapist an hour after getting divorced. "We spent five years remodeling that Sherman Oaks-adjacent house. Now he's fine with living in a box."

"Sherman Oaks-adjacent" is a phrase drummed into April's head by her real estate agent. It's Los Angeles-housing-market-speak for "$300,000 more than a house in Van Nuys". The house April owned with her husband, Morgan, was, of course, actually in Van Nuys, both when they bought it five years ago and when they sold it five weeks ago. They could never afford a home in Sherman Oaks proper.

"How so?" asks Dr. Novacheck. She's wearing bright yellow stilettos today. April keeps staring down at her own black flats. The doctor has her head tilted to the right with a patient expression pasted on her face.

April tries to catch up to the present moment. She was talking about the house . . . where was she going with this line of thinking? "Sorry. What was the question?"

"You don't have to apologize." Dr. Novacheck reminds her.

"I know. Sorry."

Shit.

Therapy is April's time. She's not supposed to apologize during her time. And if she does apologize, she's not supposed to apologize for apologizing. But, if therapy really is April's time, shouldn't she be able to be sorry without being sorry for being sorry?

April's not sure how people are supposed to feel about their therapists. Of course, she's also not sure how she's supposed to feel about divorce. Maybe the right therapist helps patients understand how they are supposed to feel about their therapists and their divorces (not the divorces of the therapists but the divorces of the patients).

Shit. Again.

Dr. Novacheck blinks at April, waiting for an answer to a question April didn't hear. April blinks back.

Therapy is working, just not in the way April expected it to. She has overdosed on analyzing her emotions since her husband announced six months ago that he wanted out of their marriage. April is sick of "sitting in her feelings" like Dr. Novacheck suggests ad nauseam. She's so annoyed by her own voice talking endlessly, not just in therapy but in her own head, that she is very ready to move on with her life.

She sold most of her worldly possessions along with the Sherman Oaks-adjacent house. And now that she signed the divorce paperwork, her value in the fourteen-year marriage will be transferred to her bank account next week.

She just has to figure out what's next. And she is suddenly very aware she's not going to figure it out in this neat little office with this neat little therapist.

She needs a messy therapist—someone who cusses. Cussing in front of someone who doesn't cuss is like trying to enjoy a juicy steak in front of a vegan. April can't trust a therapist who doesn't say shit.

She looks at the clock on the wall behind Dr. Novacheck's head. Thirty-two more minutes in this session. April isn't sure she can make it.

Dr. Novacheck presses on. "If someone said to you last year, when you were in the middle of the house remodel, 'You know Morgan would be happy in an RV,' would you have believed that?"

"You wonder if I knew my husband?"

"I wonder if he shared himself with you."

"Like, how long did he want a divorce before he told me about it?"

Dr. Novacheck chooses her words with care. "In your book, Morgan is a hero. He's almost the perfect partner. Is that really who he really is? Or, as a writer, did you create a character . . . "

"I don't think of myself as a writer."

Dr. Novacheck sits back. "I've heard you say that in interviews. But you wrote a book that was very well received."

"I wrote a story that was true, or, at least, I thought it was true at the time. I just experienced something, wrote about it, and people liked the experience I wrote about."

"Why do you think they liked it?"

"Because . . . it was a great love story. And people like to believe in great love stories."

2

L Freaking A

April takes a deep breath of fresh ocean/pot scented air just outside the front door of her therapist's office (which is Venice Beach-adjacent). She knows she won't be coming back here.

Of course, April didn't say that to Dr. Novacheck. Confrontation is not April's thing. If Dr. Novacheck was an effective therapist, she would have cured April of that by now.

Instead, April will cancel her next therapy appointment by leaving a message after hours. Then she will fail to reschedule.

She doesn't need to spend $300 dollars an hour to have someone ask her what she's going to do with her life now that she's alone, because the first thing she's going to do is save $300 an hour on therapy. As it is, she's burned through five figures of her book savings since Morgan announced he wanted a divorce.

Money wasted on lawyers, home stagers, a real estate agent, a therapist once a week, and . . . parking tickets. April can see one tucked under her windshield wiper as she approaches her car parked on Ocean Park Ave. It's a joke they named the street Ocean Park because they don't actually want you to park there. This is her fourth ticket in three months. Two of them came in one afternoon.

She passes her car and heads toward the beach. She doesn't even bother to wonder what she did to deserve the infraction. The final straw broke the camel's back weeks ago.

It was Morgan's confession that he dreamed of living in an RV that did it. In front of Dr. Novacheck, April laughed it off. How ridiculous. Midlife crisis. He'll regret it.

But the truth is, that revelation hurt April most of all—maybe even more than the divorce. They endured years of renovations to turn that damn Van Nuys house into their dream home.

Morgan used to travel with April when she appeared at romance conventions or spoke at writing conferences, but he stopped once they bought the property. Someone had to be home to manage the contractors and the deliveries as they built their dream house.

They were willing to sacrifice for the future. In one instance, they lived in the master bedroom with a mini-fridge for a nightstand, washing dishes in the bathroom sink and cooking in a microwave for four months while their kitchen was being remodeled. In another, they walked around on concrete for half a year because the flooring they wanted for the living room was back-ordered.

Five different contractors moved on to other projects instead of waiting for rare items Morgan purchased from obscure corners of the internet.

Morgan became the contractor himself for a while, but when he got offered a job in Santa Monica working with a friend, the contractor work fell to April. And going on year three of the house renovation, it became her excuse to not take traveling gigs anymore.

When her publicist would push, April would defend herself. "I can't speak at the Romance Writers Convention in Georgia next weekend, the carpenter is supposed to build the island for the kitchen." Or, "I can't go to the fan summit in Vegas this summer, they'll be working on the roof in June."

Eventually, the publicist stopped calling.

A few months after Morgan and April separated, the very final item for the house arrived; a box of one-of-a-kind kitchen cabinet handles probably forged by some gnomes in the Amazon Rainforest.

Morgan obsessed over these handles when he ordered them last year. He promised April they'd be worth the wait—just like he'd promised the flooring would be worth it, and the wallpaper from an artist in Norway, and the hand-painted frame for the bathroom mirror.

"It hurts now," he'd say, "but it'll feel so good when we have it all."

And April believed him. All those long, unsettled days living in an unfinished house would be worth it.

By the time the handles arrived, the house was already under contract with some couple who talked about painting over the Norwegian wallpaper the very first time they stepped through the front door.

When Morgan came to get his final suitcase, he and April stood in the kitchen they spent years remodeling. April pulled a handle out of the box and held it up to the hand-crafted cabinets.

Morgan shrugged as he said to his wife of fourteen years, "You can do whatever you want with them. The cabinets in the RV are corrugated board. They'd just splinter apart if I tried to add hardware."

Corrugated board. He said it so casually.

Corrugated board. Functional. Inexpensive. Ubiquitous.

April once used a porta-potty in their backyard for two weeks straight while Morgan hunted down some discontinued toilet with an extra wide (by one inch) seat. So, yes, the corrugated board was the final straw that broke April.

"Don't lie to me," she seethed through clenched teeth, her heart pounding so loud in her ears she could barely hear Morgan's response.

He seemed to read the cues well enough to know he needed to take a step back. "I'm not lying."

"You told me I can do whatever I want with these handles, but what I want to do is to shove them so far up your . . . "

April doesn't remember what was said after that. There were tears and there was fury and there was a kind of fracture down the center of her being that left her on the floor for hours after Morgan left.

There (lying in a heap on the floor of a kitchen so perfect, it once sent her to her room for four months), April discovered something life changing.

There's freedom in being at rock bottom. There's so much fear about the final straw; but once you're broken, what is there to be afraid of anymore? So in the weeks since then, April has been crawling through life mostly immune to new feelings of pain or frustration.

She walks on the sidewalk running from Venice Beach to Santa Monica. Bikers and skaters zip past her. She doesn't care.

Why doesn't she do this more? She lives in L freaking A. Why doesn't she go to the beach more? Why hasn't she learned to surf? Why doesn't she have a tan and sand calves (those muscular calves you get from walking in deep sand)?

Maybe she'll do all the things now and be all the things, if she can just decide which of the things she wants to do and be.

April spots a bench beside a coffee stand. She once met a producer here. He was one of several who wanted to option her book over the years, but it never worked out. She learned after a while to not get her hopes up.

Her friend, Yaretzi, is a screenwriter, and she calls it the 70-29-1 rule. Hollywood is seventy percent talking about what you're going to do, twenty-nine percent talking about what you have done, and one percent actually doing the shit you talk about.

It's true. Every coffee shop you go into buzzes with caffeinated chats about the future and the past. No one can afford to live in the present. Everyone is on the border of being somebody. They're all living Sherman Oaks-adjacent lives.

Several times over the years, Morgan would bring up the idea of leaving L.A. After all, April wasn't writing, and even if she was, she could do it from anywhere. But April never took Morgan's talk seriously. If he wanted to leave L.A., he wouldn't be picking out an Italian kitchen faucet made of unicorn horns.

Why didn't she listen? Why didn't she believe Morgan when he said he wanted out? And does she have the cash to buy an ice cream sandwich from the guy with the cart on the corner?

She digs in her purse. Bingo! One crumpled dollar bill and four quarters later, she's suddenly remembering that cheese danish she had earlier today as she bites into the ice cream sandwich.

Some people go full 1980s montage after their heart breaks. They work out.

They get a make-over. They buy a new wardrobe. And they are magically a new, confident person just two movie-minutes after their life falls apart.

April has taken the opposite approach. She's going through some shit, so she's eating through some shit. She undoes the top button of her pants to make room in her midsection for the ice cream. She's got no one to answer to now. She can do whatever the hell she wants.

She slips off her flats and steps barefoot onto the sand.

It's warm under her feet. It's really warm. It's burning. It's really burning. You know what?

There's a reason she doesn't do this shit. There's a reason she doesn't sit in traffic for two hours to drive to the beach to get a parking ticket and burn her feet in the sand. There's a reason she doesn't buy ice cream sandwiches at the beach that melt all over her hands and crunch with invasive grains of sand.

There's a reason she doesn't take advantage of living in Los Angeles. She doesn't actually like the beach, or standing in lines at clubs, or being promised a film option that never happens, or sitting in traffic, or redoing a home for a husband who doesn't want to live there.

Maybe it's time to live in a place where she doesn't have to pretend to live somewhere else.

3

Toby's House

My first crush was in third grade. It was all-consuming. My life soared or crashed on the smile of nine-year-old Jody Whycutt.

If you told me then, I'd be single on my thirtieth birthday and living alone in a tiny studio apartment in North Hollywood, I would have been heartbroken. To know I'd have to wait another nineteen years to have someone love me back would probably have devastated my fragile, romantic soul.

We're lucky the universe doesn't share that with us. We're lucky the top of the mountain is hidden in the clouds, so we can't see how far we have to climb.

Excerpt from *Great Expectations* by April Townsend

April sits on Yaretzi's couch, where she's been sleeping for two months, and scrolls through realty sites looking for an affordable rental anywhere in Los Angeles. An hour and a glass of wine into the search, she changes course and enters her hometown in the search box. Well, hometown might be a stretch. She enters the town where she graduated from high school.

Cleo, Texas, is a small town an hour from Dallas. Her parents moved her there, much to her disdain, just before her eighth-grade year. Five years later, she graduated high school with one-hundred-and-fifty other kids at Tiger Football Field.

Her dad was a high school baseball coach who promised the family he'd retire from coaching before his daughters reached high school. It turned out he meant he'd retire from coaching at the big city schools around the Dallas area, and instead take a job at a smaller school in a smaller town.

Having none of the talent in sports her older sister, Lilly, possessed, April didn't have the immediate friendships or the desire to like small town Texas life (with no access to bookstores, coffee shops or the indie movie theaters to which she'd grown accustomed). She retreated further into a fantasy world, which worried the hell out of her mother.

But while many kids kept drugs or sex a secret from their parents, April secretly read romance novels and watched all the Jane Austin and Bronte sisters she could find on the PBS station in her room.

She even hid in her room dressed up in her cousin's hand-me-down prom dresses, playing out fantasy scenes. All this was before the time of cosplay and avatars, before the internet, before there was a way to know other people liked to escape into fantasy worlds too.

Now she sits in the living room of Yaretzi's apartment off La Brea in Hollywood and scrolls through listings of houses in Cleo. She can afford most of them, even the nice ones. It's a welcome change of pace.

To her surprise, a very familiar house pops up in a listing. Toby's house. She used to drive by it ten times a night while listening to "Possession" by Sarah McLachlan on repeat, wishing Toby would come to the window.

Toby was a boy she hardly knew who was home-schooled, and had long hair and a pet tarantula. His parents were artists who enjoyed the short commute to Dallas and the cheap artist lofts of downtown Cleo. They moved from Cloudcroft, New Mexico when Toby got into some kind of vague trouble at school. That was the rumor anyway. And that rumor gave him the reputation of a mysterious bad boy, at least in the eyes of a small town.

How many times had she wished to see his shadow in the upstairs window? She imagined she'd pull into the driveway, he'd recognize her car (even though he didn't really even know who she was), and he'd come running out of the front door to give April her first kiss.

Her first kiss didn't actually come until the end of her senior year. Joel Tolbert was nice enough, and April wanted to be able to say she'd kissed a

11

boy. So she kissed Joel in the middle of a pasture (working hard to avoid cow patties) where her classmates met in the headlights to say goodbye under a brilliant Texas sky.

That was one thing she loved about small town Texas. It was easy to find a wide open space where no city lights, no mountains, no trees could disrupt the view of the unending stars. It was romantic actually, the setting for her first kiss, even if she and Joel had no real connection.

Morgan was April's first real love (both participants being aware they were in a relationship was helpful; poor Toby probably couldn't pick April out of a line-up). But she'd been loving boys in her head since third grade. Every year of school she'd develop some terrible new crush. First it was Jody Whycutt when she was nine. She loved him, mullet and all.

In fourth grade, it was Jonah Dryess, the only red-headed boy in her class. In fifth grade, it was Thomas Beyer who could do cool skateboard tricks; he came back again in seventh. But it was Evan Treks, who April met on the first day of eighth grade in Cleo, that made her forget all about the summer she cried at the thought of moving away from Thomas (who never gave her the least bit of attention).

Evan was the first kid to smile at her as she sat in the bleachers during first period PE at Coller Middle School. He was a student council representative tasked with helping lost souls on their first day of eighth grade. There was no soul more lost at Coller that day than that of April Townsend. At that time in her life, a new smile was all the reason she needed to move on from previous loves.

At Texas Tech, April had lots of fun with boys, but she did not find love with any of them. At least, not the reciprocal kind.

In her twenties, she moved to the big city to take on the world, but she soon discovered dating felt impossible. Dating in L.A. is like trying to catch money in one of those wind tunnel machines. It seems like potential is all around you, but every time you attempt to grasp something, you wind up with a fistful of air.

Then one night, at the last minute, April met up with her college friend, Seth, to celebrate her thirtieth birthday. When she looked up from blowing out her birthday candles, there, across the crowded bar, was Morgan. He smiled and mouthed, "Happy birthday." That hopelessly romantic kid playing dress up in her cousin's hand-me-down prom dress finally got her real-life moment.

In a lot of ways, Morgan was April's first relationship. She'd had dates, and sex, and romantic interactions, but she'd never had a relationship. She'd saved the real intimacy for a soulmate.

She believed there was one person out there somewhere meant just for her, and the only trick to finding love was finding that person. April dated enough to feel like she was trying, but as soon as she knew a guy didn't feel like a soulmate, she gave him no more energy.

She spent many years believing in that strategy because it led her to Morgan. Hell, she wrote a book telling the story of how her strategy worked; how her life settled, and peace came at last when she married her true love. She inspired women all over the world to be patient because their soulmate was out there somewhere.

But, as it turns out, Morgan wasn't even a soulmate. Or, he was a temporary soulmate, and April isn't certain if that's even a thing.

If she had more experience working on relationships before meeting Morgan, could she have seen this end coming? Could she have learned from others that love is not enough? That love comes and goes even?

Maybe everyone is inexperienced with relationships because every day is a different day and no one can ever be who they were the day before. In that way, every morning is like waking up to a stranger, both in your bed and in your mirror.

Sometimes Morgan and April's marriage was a road trip where they knew exactly where they stood and where they were headed. Sometimes they were lost and just had to trust they'd find their way back to the road they should be on. So even when the active feelings of love weren't there, the trust was.

After a while, April still trusted they'd find their way back to each other because they were meant to be. But Morgan got tired of being lost. If April recognized that discrepancy sooner, would she still have landed so hard on her ass when they split?

Maybe. That's really all April has right now—possibilities.

Maybe that's not such a bad thing.

Scrolling through the twenty-four pictures listed with Toby's old house, April's fantasy is broken. It doesn't look like it's been updated for years. It is definitely not the shiny new object of affection it was when it reigned over the Sarah McLachlan soundtracks of the 1990s. Looking at the house in photographs is like watching the movie version of a favorite book—wrong.

Something about this fantasy gone wrong creates an impulse in April she doesn't have the energy to restrain. She can fix this house. She can make it exactly what she fantasizes it to be. And she doesn't have to ask permission from anyone.

She can do whatever the hell she wants. She can put a mirror above the bed and lime green velvet curtains in the bathroom. Of course, she won't do either of those things because the first is creepy and the second is not sanitary, but she could if she wanted to and that's what matters at the moment.

She calls the number of the realtor who holds the listing in Cleo. April is startled to hear an actual voice on the other end of the line. In L.A., realtors never actually answer the phone, especially not in the evening. It's nine o'clock Texas time.

Demetria Caulder graduated two years before April. She was Demetria Jones back then. It isn't until their third phone conversation, that April makes the mental connection between Demmy Jones, who played Jack in Cleo High's Production of *Into the Woods,* and Demetria Caulder, the capable real estate agent who holds the listing for Toby's old house.

April helped with costumes for that production, mostly because her mother was devastated April hadn't found "her thing" yet. So April asked Mrs. Goodman if she needed volunteers for her next show. Really, April was hoping to just sit in the dark for a few hours fantasizing about whatever story she was living in her head. But every single time Demmy sang "Giants in the Sky", April would sneak to the alcove stage right and watch. Her performance made April want to be present for it, and that's about as high a compliment as teenage April could pay to anyone.

Adult April is sad to learn Demetria doesn't really sing anymore. And

Demetria is sad to learn April doesn't really write anymore. Of course, either of them could do those things at any time; they just don't.

But they do draw up a contract for April to purchase Toby's old house.

4

Windows

The first time April allows herself a "WTF have I done" moment is when she pulls up in the circular driveway of Toby's house . . . her house.

It looks so sad. Not at all the bright beacon of hope it had been to her in high school days. The two-story stucco home never quite fit in with the single-story wooden houses around it. That's what April loved about it when it was built. It was purposefully different.

It proudly stood out among its peers, and not in an obnoxious way like the McMansions in Los Angeles (ostentatious monstrosities taking up every square inch of a property and giving a giant middle finger to the neighbors around it). This New Mexico style house April now owns in the small town of Cleo, Texas, was once a breath of fresh air to a young, romance-obsessed high schooler who dreamed about the mysterious boy who would appear from time to time in the window.

April thought leaving the house in Van Nuys for the last time was sad, but stepping into this new house is perhaps worse. And made even worse than worse because the grief meeting her at her new front door is so unexpected.

How did she end up back where she began? Every decision she's made since the divorce seems impulsive and amateur, like a rebellious teenager. She sold most of her possessions for a few hundred bucks and took from L.A. only what she could fit in her small sedan. She bought this house on a whim. She sent a text to her parents from her hotel in Albuquerque (halfway

16

through her move) to inform them she was moving back to Cleo.

But who is she rebelling against? There's no one here but her.

April wants a distraction from her failure, but this house is empty. It's outdated. It's overwhelming. And now April has to live in it with only the faded, coral colored walls for company.

She sat, pondering where to begin, in a bare bones house in Van Nuys once, but she wasn't alone. She had her husband. They had a dream. That house seemed full of promise.

Now she sits on a small box filled with books in the middle of a house full of emptiness. Demmy was honest about the property. It has good bones but needs a lot of attention, and a lot of everything else. Furniture would be a nice start.

April focuses on her few boxes of possessions as though they might multiply if she concentrates hard enough. When April sold most of her belongings, she considered it a symbolic purging. *After all*, she'd mused, *how can you move forward when you are carrying all your baggage from the past . . . literally?*

But now, as she sits in a bare house, she misses things. It turns out having a place to sit other than the floor is a comfort. At first, April does not allow herself to cry, but when she can't motivate herself to do anything else, she cries just to occupy the time.

She'd go to sleep right now if she had a bed in her bedroom.

Is it actually a bedroom if there is no bed?

Before moving to Yaretzi's couch, April sold her mattress for $27 to a guy on Craigslist. The buyer haggled her down from $50. She bought the thing for $300 from a mattress store on Sepulveda the day Morgan moved out.

First thing she did when her husband texted her he didn't wish to be married anymore was to haul their Cal-King mattress to the curb.

Second thing she did was to drive to a chicken place on Ventura Boulevard and get their 1800 calorie taco salad—a meal Morgan always shunned because it was "three meals worth of calories disguised as a salad".

Third thing she did was head to the mattress store, buy a soft twin mattress (Morgan liked firm), strap it to the roof of her sedan, and bring it to the dream home she now lived in by herself. By the time she pulled into the driveway, the old mattress was already gone—just like the story of the couple who once slept every single night cradled together on its surface.

That soft twin mattress got April through the months of house showings, meetings with divorce attorneys, and sessions with Dr. Novacheck. And now some guy in Los Angeles is sleeping on a $27 soft twin mattress that once held the tears of a newly single gal on the Sherman Oaks border.

Mattresses move on. They find new homes and new dreams. April wonders if it's odd to hope her old mattresses get to live happy lives. Maybe that old Cal-King is holding up a couple experiencing the first electric touches of falling in love. Maybe the soft twin is . . . okay, honestly, the dude that bought a mattress for $27 is probably not doing anything super exciting on that bed, but April still chooses to hope.

On the bright side, April's room in her new home (formerly known as Toby's old house) is clean.

Empty. Clean. Whatever.

A knock at the door interrupts April mid-crying/wishing the best for her old mattresses. She's startled by the noise and moves to hide behind the box she sits on. But without curtains, Demmy peers easily through the window from outside and spots April's backside protruding from behind a box.

Demmy raises her voice so April can hear it through the glass. "Are you supposed to be a box with a human ass or a human with a box head?"

April keeps her head down. "I'm not here."

"Oh good. Then I'll just get the key out of the lockbox."

Shit. April forgot there's still one of those realtor key boxes fastened to the handle on her garage door. She opens the front door just as Demmy retrieves the house key from the lockbox.

"Oh!" Demmy feigns surprise. "I didn't think you were home."

"Sorry," April shrugs, "I'm a little . . ."

The words catch in her throat.

Demmy puts a reassuring hand on April's arm, but doesn't otherwise acknowledge the tears in her eyes. "I brought you a welcome basket. It has tea from a shop downtown. I could make you a cup."

To April's amazement, she hears herself say, "That would be great." And she feels herself open the door wider to allow Demmy in. It's not every day procrastination knocks on your door. Usually one has to go looking for it.

In the kitchen, April stares at the boxes on the floor realizing she has no idea where a tea kettle or cups would be or if she even has any. She vaguely remembers putting a kettle in a box that may have gone to charity.

"Better yet," says Demmy, "let me take you right to the source."

Demmy chatters on the short drive to Tea'd Off, a cute little tea and coffee shop downtown, and April finds herself grateful for the noise. Demmy suggests a drink with lavender and honey as she leaves April at a table on the front patio. April is thankful for the excuse of sunshine to wear her sunglasses. She suspects her old friend chose the outdoor spot for that exact purpose.

Downtown is so different from when she lived here years ago. It was a ghost town then, with only a few stores open. There was a department store, though. Lilly worked there one Christmas wrapping presents. It was like walking back into the nineteen sixties.

Now there is a Main Street Committee with a dedicated board working to bring in new businesses and keep the old buildings up. Demmy explained in the home buying process that people even drive in from Dallas for a day of classic Americana. Downtown is now a mix of the nostalgia for the days when families drove in from their farms to spend the whole weekend visiting civilization and a modern sensibility with clever names like Tea'd Off.

The day is an unusually beautiful fall day for Texas, or so April thinks. She just remembers the terrible heat of her teen years. Was fall always nice like this?

Demmy appears with two steaming cups of tea. She keeps talking about Cleo and all there is to see and do while April's mind wanders. The distraction from the house full of boxes and sad colored walls is welcome.

Several people enter and exit the tea shop. They exchange pleasantries with Demmy and take long glances at April. Their eyes wonder who this stranger is, but their mouths are too polite to ask.

"Around here, if you see someone you don't recognize, you don't say so," says Demmy. "Chances are you should know them and you'll embarrass yourself for not knowing. You didn't want me to introduce you?"

"No," April is quick to answer.

"I didn't think so," says Demmy. "They'll figure it out soon enough."

A tall, slender man in slacks and a nice sweater eyes April as he opens the front door. He looks familiar to her, but she can't place him. As he exits with a cup of coffee, he interrupts Demmy's monologue on farm fresh eggs versus store bought.

"April?" the man smiles.

"Oh my god. Joel?"

For a moment, April pictures the seventeen-year-old who first kissed her under the moonlight of a Texas pasture. He is taller than April remembers. She'll find out from Demmy later that he grew so much in college, no one recognized him at the ten-year reunion. He's handsome. Very handsome.

"You're visiting?" he asks.

April and Demmy exchange a look. April answers, "Yes. What about you? You live here?"

"No."

April feels her heart sink a bit.

"My husband and I live in Dallas."

Her heart takes a nosedive. That could be one reason they had no connection when they kissed.

Joel raises his eyebrows as he looks at April. She takes it as an acknowledgment of their history. Then he moves on, "But Daniel and I own an antique store down the street and that keeps us tied here all the time."

"Good for you," says April. She means it on all fronts.

"Come see us sometime. Daniel works almost every day and I'm here when I can be."

Demmy interjects, "Joel is a big-time lawyer in Dallas."

"Not big time," Joel says.

"He's listed as one of the top twenty lawyers in Texas by *Dallas Magazine*."

"Yes, well . . . yes," he concedes.

"And April, of course, is . . ." Demmy doesn't have to finish the sentence. Joel knows his classmate's claim to fame.

"Yes. I'm very aware of your success. I loved the book."

April forces herself to keep her smile even though her stomach twists at the thought of Joel reading her book—the thought of anyone reading it, really. A year ago, she was so proud of the book. It was the thing in her life she was most proud of. Then she was a headline for a news cycle.

Romance Writer Gets Divorced.

Mercifully, Joel seems in a hurry. He invites April to visit his shop sometime as he politely exits. April doesn't remember much of the rest of her visit with Demmy. Is this how it's going to be here? People knowing her book, and knowing about her divorce and knowing where she lives. Why didn't she move to the middle of nowhere and start all over? Why did she come back to where people would know the truth already?

Amateur.

Demmy drops April off and shouts to her as April keys into her front door, "Start with your bed. That's what my grandmother told me after my divorce. Put your bed together first so you have a place to go when you're too tired to do the rest."

That would be helpful advice if April had a bed.

She drags herself to Walmart for a blow up mattress and some cereal for dinner. She freezes in front of the milk refrigerator; not knowing what kind to reach for.

Years ago, before she was married, April drank two percent milk. Morgan liked whole milk because it helped him bulk up. It never made sense to buy two kinds. So for fourteen years, April just used whole milk in tiny amounts to avoid the high fat intake. But now? Now she can get whatever-the-hell dairy percentage she desires.

Back home, she blows up her new mattress, has cereal in a plastic bowl filled to the brim with two percent milk and hangs an old sheet as a curtain over her bedroom window upstairs. It's the same window teenage April drove by over and over, hoping to see the dark figure of Toby appear.

Once, she'd even been brave enough to turn around in the driveway, thinking the headlights reflecting in his bedroom window might draw Toby's attention to the white Toyota Supra and the girl behind the wheel waiting for her first kiss.

Now April is the dark figure in the window looking out on a quiet street.

5

Haunting Tables

I'm often creeped out by the leading men in romance movies. They're too good looking and too intense. I wonder how the actresses on the receiving end of their smoldering looks manage to suppress their fight-or-flight instincts. These actors are just trying too hard. Intensity does not equal connection.

Of course, in my single twenties, I wouldn't have minded at least a little intensity or a hint of a smoldering look. Hell, I would have been satisfied with direct eye contact for three seconds.

Living in Los Angeles, I became accustomed to never being the center of men's attention. I grew used to men casually focusing on me while keeping their peripheral vision searching the room for anyone with more beauty and more power.

When I first moved to this city, I'd try to follow their gaze, assuming something must be happening for them to turn their focus mid-conversation. But I learned it was better to not know what shiny new object captured their attention. And I learned to not invest too much in conversations or in expectations. I didn't realize it at the time, but I began to get the message I wasn't interesting enough, or pretty enough or powerful enough to keep a man's attention.

So when I was blowing out the candles on my thirtieth birthday cake and an attractive man sitting on the other side of the bar mouthed, "Happy birthday," to me, I didn't trust him to mean it. Because I didn't trust I deserved his attention.

When he came over to talk to me, I kept waiting for him to glance over my shoulder and discover someone more worthy of his time.

But Morgan only looked at me. And not in the creepy, intense way of a romantic lead, but in a sincere way. Not like he was forcing himself to stay focused on me, but like it didn't even occur to him to look elsewhere.

Excerpt from *Great Expectations* by April Townsend

In the morning, April rewards herself for surviving the first night in a new house (and a sort-of-new town) with a trip downtown for tea. It's harder to find a parking spot on Wednesdays when Downtown Baptist serves a free lunch. April parks a couple blocks away from Tea'd Off. As she walks toward her destination, she passes a very cute antique storefront.

She opens the door to Antic Witties. The smell of candied apples greets her as she steps inside. She assumes the aroma originates from the candle burning on the counter.

A man with bright blue eyes looks up from the register. This must be Daniel. Good for Joel. His husband has a warm and inviting energy with the good looks to match. April likes him instantly but tries to restrain her enthusiasm so as not to scare away his friendship.

"Welcome. Can I help you find something?" Daniel asks.

"I'm a friend of Joel. I just came to look around."

"Oh good," he grins. "Help yourself. The first room to your right here is English antiques and the last room is American. Household goods are behind me and the wedding registry room is there." He points to a room past the household goods.

"Ah, I'll start back here."

April heads toward the household goods, stopping at a table of neatly arranged candles.

"Are you a fan of antiques?" Daniel asks.

"They're beautiful." April should stop here. Of course, she doesn't. "I just can't settle at the thought of owning something with a story I don't know. Makes me feel superstitious."

Daniel isn't offended, but he takes a moment before he answers. "Interesting. It's the story I don't know that makes me like antiques. I like knowing these pieces get to outlive our use for them and start a new life even long after we're gone."

"That's funny," April stops sniffing a lemon scented candle, "I was just thinking of that yesterday. But not about antiques. It was mattresses."

Daniel's eyebrows raise. "Mattresses?"

April reconsiders sharing this concept with a stranger she will run into frequently around town. She attempts to cut the sharing short. "It's not the same thing you're saying but kind of along those lines. How long have you and Joel had this shop?"

"Wait, no. You can't do that," Daniel says.

April puts down the candle she just picked up, not sure what she's doing wrong.

"No. You can sniff the candle. I like that one, it's vanilla lavender. But you can't tell me you were thinking of mattresses starting over again and then not finish the thought. I'm intrigued."

April sighs. "I don't even know if it makes sense. But yesterday, I just got to hoping my two old mattresses have found good new homes. Like, new stories that are . . . that have happy endings."

She immediately realizes her mistake.

Thankful Daniel is not a single, straight male she wants to impress, she laughs. "I heard it. I heard it as soon as I said it."

Daniel is delighted. "I was gonna say, doesn't every mattress deserve a happy ending?" He lifts himself to sit on the counter by the register. "What did you do with the old mattresses? Because if you took them to the dump, their second story is probably like a dystopian novel."

"No. No dump. They both found a new home. The twin mattress, which was too soft by the way . . ."

"Good to know," Daniel nods.

"Was bought by a guy online who talked me down from $50 to $27."

"Why $27?"

"I did not ask questions."

"Yeah, I hate to be a pessimist, but that mattress is not getting any kind of happy ending."

April laughs, a genuine laugh. Like, a really decent laugh. How long has it been? Long enough to notice the odd sensation of her stomach muscles pulling in with joy.

Daniel seems satisfied he elicited that response. "But everything has a story, doesn't it?" He picks up the red candy apple candle burning near him. Careful to avoid spilling the melted wax, he examines the label. "Even something new. For example, this is Candy. She was born in a family-owned factory in Fredericksburg, Texas. She smells like a fall festival and she's looking for the right match to light her fire."

"Okay," April plays along, "now tell me the story of this table." She indicates the antique table holding the candles.

"It comes from England," Daniel begins.

"Got it," says April.

"And it was built in the late 1800s."

"Interesting."

"And it was built for . . . people . . . to eat meals on . . ."

"Fascinating," April smiles as though she's proven some point.

"It is!" Daniel insists. "Not knowing its full story is what makes it fascinating. Perhaps it belonged to a family who took in a traveling stranger one night, and the daughter fell in love with the stranger right across this table. And they had twenty kids who all became doctors, saved a billion lives and found a cure for cancer."

April traces a scratch on the table with her finger. She gives her own version of its history. "It could have belonged to a local doctor, and one night there was a knock on his door. A man stumbled in bleeding from a bear attack. The doctor hoisted the man on this table to perform emergency surgery and the man bled all over it. And now he haunts it."

"The bear-man haunts that table?"

"The doctor haunts this table. The bear-man survived. And he goes on to find a cure . . . for bears."

"Oh, I did not see that coming."

April shrugs. "We already established I like happy endings."

Daniel looks surprised by April's humor, but he's smiling. "Yes, we did."

"So now," April opens the lid to the vanilla lavender candle and interrupts herself. "Oh, that is really nice."

"I told you."

April puts the lid on the candle and refocuses. "You have to tell me how long this shop has been here so we can change subjects."

"This shop has been here since I was in high school. Joel and I bought it about five years ago." Daniel hops off the counter and walks toward April with his hand extended. "I'm Daniel."

April takes his calloused hand for a shake as she tries to find something familiar in his features. He looks somewhere close to her age. If Daniel went to high school in Cleo, then April might know him.

"April," she says as she takes him in. He senses she's searching for something.

"Are you from here?" he asks.

"Sort of. I graduated from high school here. My maiden name is Townsend. Well, it still is, I didn't change it after . . . "

Daniel's face lights up with understanding. He cuts her off before she has to try to finish that sentence. "You're Coach's daughter."

"Yes." Goodness, it has been many years since she's been recognized as Coach's daughter. Odd how that association brings equal feelings of pride and resentment.

"You have a sister, right?"

"Yes, Lilly. She was two grades above me."

"So you were the one who didn't play softball?"

"Correct." April suppresses the urge to talk about her accomplishments. There was a time, not long ago, she would have casually brought up the fact she authored a very popular book. There was a time she was very proud of that fact, even if she saw it as a novelty—her fifteen minutes of fame rather than a result of her talent. Now, she'd rather people not recognize her as the author of *Great Expectations* (a title she regrets deeply), because her book about her real life love is forever attached to her real life divorce.

"I didn't mean it in a bad way. I didn't play sports either. I'm Daniel Rayburn."

"Yes," April smiles as though that name jogs her memory. It doesn't. Before she shows him she can't remember who he is (and before he remembers anything else about April), she picks up the vanilla lavender candle. "I'll get this one."

"Okay, just to warn you, that candle is worth $20 more than a soft twin mattress."

April blinks, not sure she understands. She flips the candle over, looking for a price to confirm. Yep. It's a $47 candle. "Wow, thanks for the warning. I really don't . . . is the wick made of gold?"

Daniel shakes his head. "No. No. The gold wicks are in the back. This is our sterling silver collection."

"I . . . might have to come back for this another day."

"I hope so," Daniel says as he walks April to the front and pulls the door open for her.

"It was nice to meet you, Daniel."

"You too, April."

She gets a few steps away from the door before he calls after her, "April?" She turns back to him. "I'm pretty sure there aren't any bears in England."

6

Balls of Steel

Do bears live in England? April searches her phone for the answer while crossing the street half a block from the antique store. She squints as the sun reflects off her screen and then, just as she steps up on the other side of Main Street and rounds the statue on the corner, something happens.

She can't say what. It feels like the world is chaos around her. Nothing quite makes sense. There are balls in her face. Steel balls. A sack of steel balls?

Yes. April has run headfirst into the metal statue of former Cleo state champion basketball coach, Ron Basham, which stands at the corner of Main Street and 6th. With the blinding sun bouncing off his metal face and a sack of steel basketballs slung over his shoulder, Coach Basham is still a force to be reckoned with.

April looks around to see if anyone noticed she just knocked the hell out of her head on Coach's ball sack. No one's walking on the street, thank goodness, because this is embarrassing as hell. April needs to sit down, but she won't do it in public. She has to make it to her car, but if she heads back across the street, she'll pass Antic Witties again. She opts to walk a block down, past The Diner which has been a staple of Downtown Cleo since the fifties, and cross the street at 5th Ave to get back to her car.

As she staggers the block, she attempts to pull off the look of a casual stroll. She slows down as she passes The Diner and politely smiles at the patrons sitting on the tiny patio. Nothing to see here–definitely not a woman who just ran headfirst into balls.

Sure, yes, the buildings are fading in and out of her peripheral vision. In fact, it's like lights shutting off from the outside in. Just as her tunnel vision is in full effect, April slumps into the seat of her car and closes her eyes for a second . . . or a minute or two.

She wakes up to a phone ringing. It's Demmy.

April hits the speaker icon and answers the phone by saying, "You're never going to believe what I'm doing."

"Running into statues downtown," Demmy says.

April looks around. "Where are you?!"

"At my office, but my assistant is picking up lunch at The Diner and said you slammed into Coach B and then staggered down the street like a drunk."

"Shit."

"Are you okay? Where are you now?"

"In my car in front of the antique store."

"There are a dozen antique stores downtown. Be more specific."

"Daniel's place. Joel's place. Does The Diner still have that potato salad?"

"Yes, I'll bring you some if you survive. There's a doctor's office right around the corner from you."

Silence. Demmy starts to worry. "April? April, can you hear me?"

April wakes up to someone knocking on her window. A phone is ringing. A man's arm reaches across her and picks up the ringing phone on her passenger seat. "I'm here. She's awake. I'll call you back."

April's eyes try to focus on the man standing on her driver's side. He has her car door open. He's holding her phone and looking down at her with concern.

"Daniel?" April squeaks.

His face shows an ounce of relief as he kneels on the pavement beside her. April tries to focus. "Don't!" she slurs, "Don't get on the ground. You'll ruin your nice pants."

Daniel sets a first aid kit on April's lap. "Don't worry about my pants. Let's worry about your head. I'm going to pull your legs out of the car, okay?"

Before April can comprehend his words, Daniel scoops his right arm under her knees and gently sets her feet down on the pavement in front of him. He takes gauze out of the first aid kit as he chats.

"Demmy called. Said you took a good knock to the head."

"It was Coach Basham's balls."

Daniel presses his lips together to avoid smiling at the expense of April's impaired cognitive abilities. He nods as he puts the gauze in April's palm and wraps his fingers around her wrist, lifting her hand to a spot above her right eye. "Keep that there for me."

April pulls the gauze down to see it's covered in blood. "Oh no." The only thing more embarrassing than running into a statue and being rescued by the dude she just met is having tears fill her eyes.

Daniel gives her knee a reassuring pat. "It's not bad. You might just need a couple stitches or some glue," he says as he pulls on a pair of gloves from the kit and tears off the top of the alcohol wipe package.

April can't help but think it looks like he's opening a condom package. She will not mention this. She will not . . .

"Looks like a condom package."

Daniel looks up in surprise. He pulls out the wipe. "No. Just an alcohol wipe. Different kind of protection. Protection from germs."

"I almost got knocked out, not knocked up. Right?" April laughs at her own joke.

"That's right," Daniel responds. He is not laughing.

April's musings would be charming if a head injury did not cause them. Daniel tries to clean up some of the blood, but it's hard to see the extent of the wound. "I've got a doctor friend around the corner. Think you can walk there if I help?" Daniel asks.

"I don't need help!" April exclaims as she rushes to stand and smacks her head against the doorjamb of her car.

As they walk to the clinic, Daniel insists on having April's arm propped around his shoulders. He tries to keep her talking.

"How do you know Demmy?" he asks. "School?"

"Yes, originally. Then she sold me a house."

He looks up at her. "Really? Here in town?"

"Yes. The stucco house on Hickory Street."

"That's a nice house. It deserves someone who will take care of it."

"Are you friends with Demmy?" April asks.

"Yes. Demmy is somewhat of a celebrity around here, but I'm lucky to get to call her my friend."

"Mmmmm," April rests her head on Daniel's shoulder.

"She's good at keeping secrets. A celebrity author moves in and Demmy doesn't say a word about it."

April looks at Daniel. He has two heads. She chooses one to focus on and says, "You looked me up."

"I did. As soon as you left the store. I thought it was you who wrote the book, but I didn't want to embarrass myself if I was wrong."

"Ha, well, joke's on me, because now I'm the one who's embarrassed."

"Hey," Daniel smiles, "I've seen three other people walk into Coach's balls since I took over the shop."

"That's not what I'm embarrassed about. I mean, it is for sure. Who puts a ball sack on a statue?! But it's the book I'm talking about."

"It was a success, right?"

"It sold a lot of copies," April says.

"I would call that a success."

"But you said you like antiques because they are a mystery. My story isn't a mystery to anybody."

An hour later, April exits the exam room with a glued forehead to find both Demmy and Daniel waiting in the lobby. And by the looks on their faces, they've been talking about her.

Daniel moves to shake hands with Dr. White, who glued Humpty Dumpty back together again. Demmy threads her arm through April's.

"How about a drink?" Demmy offers.

"No drinking," says Dr. White. "And no driving. And someone should check on her while she sleeps. She probably has a mild concussion."

Apparently, HIPAA laws don't exist in Cleo.

Demmy takes April home. After picking up some potato salad and a side of saltines from The Diner (per Demmy's instructions), Daniel drives April's car to her house. She tries to appear grateful even though she's mortified by the events of the last two hours.

When Demmy and Daniel watch her take a bite of potato salad, April has had all she can stand of being taken care of by semi-strangers.

"You have to go. Thank you for everything, but you have to go now."

Daniel stands up from April's kitchen table (a couple of boxes stacked on top of each other with other boxes for chairs). "I'll go," he offers.

"Take her with you," April points at Demmy. Demmy tries to protest but finally agrees to leave after April sets an hourly alarm on her phone and promises to text Demmy every time it goes off.

When Daniel opens the front door to exit, he sees a large, heavy box blocking his path outside. He drags the box in.

"Oh, that's the dresser I ordered," says April with a fork full of potato salad waiting to enter her mouth.

Daniel hauls the box to her bedroom upstairs and notices April only has a blow up mattress. He pulls a business card out of his wallet and sets it on top of the dresser box. As he leaves the house, he tells April to call him if she needs help putting the dresser together.

When the two well-meaning nurses leave, April is relieved to be alone in the quiet of her house. It's the first time the silence of the house feels like a comfort.

She can't watch anything on her computer. It gives her a headache, which she has to admit may well be a sign of a concussion. So she focuses wholly on the joys of The Diner's potato salad.

It tastes like high school.

7

Doing Dishes

Right after Morgan and I got engaged, I attended a bachelorette party for a coworker. It was at a strip club in this huge warehouse space off Vine Avenue near Hollywood. These very fit and oiled up guys performed elaborate scenes. One dancer was a firefighter on a fire escape. Another was a judge in a courtroom scenario. There was a lineman on an electrical pole who used it like a stripper pole. It was much more extravagant than I ever imagined a male strip club to be.

The crowd was mostly women there for milestone birthday celebrations or bachelorette parties. The woman at the table next to us was celebrating her divorce. We were all having fun, being raucous.

But then the lights come up and there's this kind of average-build guy wearing a t-shirt and jeans just standing in front of a small counter. The crowd is quiet, trying to figure out what's happening as the guy wheels this counter around so the crowd can see it's a sink full of dishes. And the crowd erupts, like goes absolutely wild when this title graphic pops up on the screen in the background that reads, "Doing the dishes."

So I'm thinking this guy is about to hump some bowls, but he proceeds to just wash the dishes . . . for ten minutes. At one point he gets under the sink to "fix" a leak and comes up with his shirt all wet. So, of course, he takes the shirt off. And the guy is not built like the judge or the lineman. He doesn't look like he works out four hours a day. Not unattractive at all, but not a body you'd look at twice if you jogged by it.

He opens a drawer and pulls out a pink ruffled apron with a big pocket across the front. As he slips it over his head and ties it in the back, the audience loses their minds. Then the guy just carefully continues to wash the dishes. He takes his time with each dish. When his fist, holding the sponge, slowly disappears inside a coffee cup, the crowd goes berserk, but I'm not even sure it's an intentional sexual gesture because it's done in such a pedestrian manner.

The song, "This Woman's Work", starts playing over the speakers. I'm thinking this has to be one of the most surreal experiences of my life. For the big finale, the guy holds up the last bowl from the sink. It's a large serving bowl which makes it easier to see the details of the design. The bowl is a soft yellow with this delicate blue ribbon rimming the top edge. Two little blue birds intertwine where the ribbon meets from each side. It looks like it belongs in the modern kitchen of a little country house. This guy dries it with a red tea towel that's been hanging from the back of his pants.

He's gentle. He takes his time. He wipes off every spot of water. He handles it like it's precious. And I'm so enthralled, it takes me a moment to notice that it's silent in the audience now.

The divorced woman at the next table is wiping tears from her eyes. Other women have their hands over their hearts. Many have these wistful expressions.

So the song ends and this guy bows and the crowd leaps to their feet, giving him a standing ovation as he moves to the edge of the stage and sets down the bowl. Women throw tips in it. It's filled up in minutes. And the guy walks the rim of the stage touching hands with women who are reaching up to him like he's a famous singer just finishing a concert. They're handing him money that he's stuffing into the apron pocket. But he's not working these women—not giving them lap dances or letting them touch his biceps (which aren't really all that impressive).

He's connecting with them. Acknowledging them. Listening.

There's a blackout. Black Sabbath blares. A guy dressed as a cop rides a motorcycle onstage. He takes off his helmet, and the crowd erupts in fun, drunken debauchery again.

Two weeks after witnessing this event, Morgan and I are at Macy's registering for our wedding china. I'm looking at a wall full of dish sets in various patterns and there it is, a light yellow dish set with the blue ribbon rim that ends in the shape of two birds intertwined.

Morgan and I did not choose that pattern for obvious reasons. We chose a set of practical, solid colored place settings instead.

Even so, I think of that stripper every time I do the dishes. He understood, maybe too late for his own marriage, women long to share the work of life more than they long to share a bed.

Excerpt from *Great Expectations* by April Townsend

April does as she is told. She wakes up every hour to text Demmy. Sometimes she sends an emoji, sometimes a GIF, sometimes autocorrect ridden texts; the strangest being a text at 4 a.m. that reads, *I have vaginitis.* April could not recall the next day what it was she was trying to text her friend at 4 a.m., but she was fairly certain it was not intended to be about her nether regions or any kind of "itis".

After startling herself in the mirror during a late-night bathroom break, April sees her black eye for the first time. She messages Demmy a pirate emoji.

She sends a final text at 7 a.m., wishing Demmy a good day and assuring her friend she has survived the night. She rolls over and goes back to sleep.

A knock on the door startles her awake. Her phone says it's 11:30 a.m.

April wriggles off her blow up mattress and throws on a robe as she heads to the front door. To her surprise, she comes face to face with her sister, Lilly. It's been two years since they have seen one another.

"You just answer the door?" chastises Lilly. You don't think murderers . . . oh my god!" Lilly puts her index finger under April's chin and lifts it to the light to better see the black and blue around her sister's eye. "What the hell happened?"

"I ran into Coach Bashum's . . . statue." April avoids adding the ball sack detail for the moment. "What's that?" April asks, referring to a brown bag in Lilly's hand.

"It's potato salad from The Diner."

April smiles, "Come on in."

In the kitchen, April attempts to find some cups from random boxes stacked about as she asks her sister what she's doing in Cleo.

"You got divorced and bought a house in a town you hated growing up in," Lilly answers. "I'm here to see if you're sane. Which, by the looks of you, the answer is probably no."

"I didn't hate it here. I just didn't know myself here. Did they give you crackers?" April sounds panicked. The potato salad from The Diner has to be eaten with saltines. That's the way it is and always has been and forever shall be. April doesn't see any crackers in the bag. Lilly reaches into her purse and pulls out a handful.

April feels relieved. "I really did run into a statue. They have them all over downtown," April assures her sister. "I saw a doctor. Some friends took care of me."

Lilly sets her purse down, takes the potato salad from April's hand and sets it down too. Then, she pulls her little sister into a hug. It occurs to April, as she is wrapped in Lilly's arms, this is the first hug she's felt in weeks. The daily contact she took for granted while she was married is now a novelty.

Lilly must know it too, because she holds on for an uncomfortably long time. As April tries to squirm out of the tight hold, Lilly squeezes tighter. "I'm waiting for you to relax."

"Well, it's not going to happen while you're hugging me."

"Just drop those shoulders. They're holding up your ears right now."

April relents, relaxing her sloped shoulders with a sigh. They are indeed up higher than they should be. She wonders how long they've been there.

After enjoying their diner treat, Lilly insists on helping April unpack some boxes (even though April tries desperately to procrastinate). Yes, there have been times over the last couple days April regrets selling most of her belongings, but she hasn't even had the drive to unpack the few boxes she has.

When they've finished unpacking the scant items for the kitchen, Lilly announces she has a box of April's dishes in the car. It takes April a moment to understand. Her stomach sinks.

Right after April and Morgan married, they lived in a small, one-bedroom apartment in North Hollywood. There was only room in the kitchen cabinets for four place settings from their wedding registry. The other two settings, plus the serving platters, were brought to April's parents' house. They've spent all these years in the Townsend's attic above the garage in Spring, TX.

By the time April and Morgan had a kitchen big enough to fit the extra dishes, they were getting a divorce.

"Don't bring them in the house," April insists.

"What? Why? You have plenty of room in the kitchen cabinets," Lilly scoffs.

"Which I don't want to contaminate with old associations." April's tone makes it clear she's done arguing.

Lilly is not. "Morgan never even touched these. They're still in their original packaging, packed inside a box that's been sealed for fourteen years."

"We should donate them," says April.

"Why? These are like new."

April is suddenly annoyed her sister is here, invading her space and questioning what she puts in it. "Lilly, one of the few upsides to divorce is the freedom to not have to explain myself to anyone."

"I'm trying to help you be practical. You don't have anything."

"I have my choices." The volume of her own words surprises April. She lowers her voice. "You may not understand them—this house, or the dishes, or any other wacky decision I've made in the last few months. I'm not even saying I understand them, but I am enjoying having choices and making decisions for which I am the only one who suffers the consequences."

"Your happiness matters to me and to Mom and Dad." Lilly takes a step toward her sister. "If you are hurting, we're hurting too."

"Don't do that to me."

"Do what?"

"Make me responsible for your hurt or for the things you choose to worry about. This is why I don't tell you stuff, because you make it about you."

"I do not make it about me. I'm trying to help."

"So that you feel better. You're trying to help me so you can feel better about my situation."

38

The hurt registers on Lilly's face.

April backs off. "I don't want to fight. Let me buy you dinner."

"I should get home." Lilly gathers her belongings. "Trey will have a hard time getting Archie to bed."

"Surely he can handle it for one night," April begins, but stops when Lilly looks at her. Talking about their marriages has never been possible for the sisters. They instinctively play defense or offense when the subject arises. Lilly always assumed April had an ideal marriage with Morgan. All she knew about their relationship, she'd read in April's book—like hundreds of others.

Lilly would have loved a proper wedding registry. Instead, she got her parent's hand-me-down dishes her mom collected from the local grocery store by earning points toward a set of china every time she bought groceries in the late 1980s.

Instead of place settings and blenders, Lilly got a baby registry.

She married Trey when she was pregnant with their daughter, Kate. The wedding wasn't a big celebration. There was no money for a honeymoon. There isn't much romantic about moving in with someone while you're vomiting every morning. The most elaborate part of the wedding festivities was the bachelorette party April threw for Lilly in L.A. Lilly forbade April to talk about her in the book. So when April wrote about the party, she referred to Lilly as a coworker.

Lilly never understood why anyone would want to hear about a stripper washing dishes, but that story was the part of her sister's book Lilly's friends mentioned to her the most.

Lilly was proud of her sister, of course. But she was struggling to raise a baby and figure out a rushed marriage while her sister had a fairy tale wedding followed by a hit book about her fairy tale romance. Lilly worked hard to be gracious and happy for her sister. She mostly succeeded.

There have been years where Lilly and Trey weren't sure if they were in love, but they were sure they were committed to their family. Now, they have three kids. Kate and Nathan are in high school and Archie is starting kindergarten. Archie was "an unexpected blessing" as Lilly sometimes refers to him. At first, she feared raising another baby might put the final nail in the coffin of her marriage to Trey. But they are surviving. There are even days they like each other.

If Lilly was honest with herself, she'd admit to feeling smug when she found out about the divorce. April's marriage wasn't so perfect after all. And Lilly's marriage wasn't so bad after all. So, in some awful way of the ego, Lilly was relieved when her sister, the great romance author, failed at marriage. The guilt of that relief is what motivates her to "fix" things for her sister now.

April tries another way to make amends with Lilly. "I'll text Trey and tell him I'm kidnapping you for the night. He wouldn't want you driving so long in the dark, anyway."

Lilly nods even though she still hasn't fully let go of the accusations from her sister, probably because they are true.

After dinner at Buckneye's, a restaurant run by a chef from Australia who married a local, the sisters settle into April's bedroom for the night. Happy to not be alone in her empty house, April crawls into a sleeping bag on the floor.

"You really can have the blowup mattress," Lilly says as she enters the room with freshly brushed teeth (she carries a toothbrush and toothpaste in her purse at all times).

"That's alright," says April. "You're my guest."

As Lilly passes the box with the dresser inside, she stops to look at Daniel's business card. She turns off the overhead light before crawling onto the small blowup mattress. "What was Daniel Rayburn doing in your bedroom?"

"Just bringing the dresser upstairs. He's one of the people who took me to the doctor for this beauty." April points to her black eye.

Lilly looks either horrified or delighted. It's hard to tell in the pale glow of the nightlight plugged into the wall behind her. "Daniel saw you run into Coach's sack?!"

Over margaritas at dinner, April confessed the whole truth of her encounter with Coach B. Lilly laughed so hard, margarita came out of her nose.

"No, but it was still horrifying. Demmy called him to come check on me after I passed out in my car."

"Is he still cute? I had such a crush on him in high school. When he was in the talent show, I cheated and voted for him twice."

"What was his talent?"

"Caricatures. He brought Mrs. Goodman onstage and then drew her on a poster that faced the audience."

"That's an odd talent for a high school kid."

Lilly shrugs. "He was an odd guy, I guess. I'm not sure he cared what other people thought, which made everybody like him. It's weird how that works."

"Was he in your class?"

"No. One grade above me. He must have been a senior your freshman year. I was so sad when he married the twirler. What was her name?"

April's brow furrows. "He married a girl?"

"Yes. The twirler. The one who did all that crazy shit with fire. She won all those competitions."

"The one with the leg trick?" April circles her arm like a leg flying through the air.

"Yes. I don't know why I can't remember her name. Anyway, Daniel proposed to her during halftime at a football game. "

"This can't be the same Daniel."

"Yes," Lilly sounds exasperated. "You never pay attention. I swear. Everyone knew Daniel. He had a different given name I think, but he went by Daniel. His brother was in your class."

"Who?"

"Uh, the guy, the attorney in Dallas who did all those cases."

Uh oh. April doesn't like where this is going.

Lilly continues to try to get her sister on board. "The guy in your class. The guy who's married to the city councilman in Dallas."

Double uh oh.

April still can't allow herself to accept this revelation. "You don't mean Joel Tolbert?"

"Yes! Thank you."

April is desperate for her sister to be mistaken about this. Joel and

41

Daniel are not brothers. They are husbands. Because she did not talk to a heterosexual stranger of a man about her discarded matrimonial mattress, then have him take care of her after she ran into a statue's balls.

"They have different last names." April points out.

Lilly is undeterred. "Different dads. But I think Joel's dad raised them both. I don't know if Daniel's father was in the picture."

April is glad it's dark. Otherwise, it would be hard to hide her mortified expression. Goodness gracious. What all crazy shit did she talk about with Daniel? Her insecurities about her book. Not being able to afford a candle. Surgery performed on a table. And, of course, ball sacks. And, just for good measure, a condom package in the form of an alcohol wipe. But at least she didn't make several references to happy endings over the course of their conversation!

She rolls over so her back is to her sister as she squeezes her eyes shut and tries to remember what Joel said that made her confuse his brother for his spouse.

Joel said he was married to a man and they live in Dallas. Then he said something like, "Daniel and I own an antique store in town. Daniel is at the store a lot." April assumed Daniel is the husband, but Joel must have assumed April would know Daniel as his brother. But she didn't—perhaps because, as Lilly says, April doesn't pay attention. And now she's made a total ass out of herself.

"April?" The way Lilly says her name makes it clear April has gone into her own head again and missed something in the outside world.

"Yes?" April responds.

"I asked you if Daniel's still married."

"Oh." April does her best to sound casual. "I thought he was married, but now I'm not sure." April really hopes he is not, because if he is . . . she talked to a married man about happy endings.

"Mmm," Lilly grunts. It's the kind of grunt that hints at finality, so April hopes that's the end of any conversation for the night.

But she's not so lucky.

Just as April is about to fall into sleep (or at least pretend she is) Lilly speaks.

"Do you remember how you'd sneak into my room every night after Mom and Dad went to sleep?"

"Yes," says April. "You used to set the alarm so I'd wake up before them and get back to my own bed."

"Why did they care so much if we slept in the same room?"

"I don't know. It could be they just hated I was so afraid to be alone. They worried I'd never grow out of it if they indulged me," April says.

"Did you grow out of it?" Lilly asks.

April rolls over to look at her sister. "Well, I'm not the one that drove in from Houston to sleep in my sister's bed."

Lilly stares at the ceiling. "I remember once we fought all day, but you still came into my room that night."

"I remember that. We fought about the gummy bears."

"Yes! You licked one and handed it to me."

"I remember." April laughs. "I licked it and stuck it on your shirt."

"Then you threw the rest of them across the room and told me if I wanted more, I could go get them."

"I was such a brat."

"And Mom and Dad never believed me. They thought you were this perfect little angel."

"A perfect little codependent angel."

The sisters fall silent for a beat. April breaks it.

"Morgan and I fought about candy once. I loved these chocolate covered strawberries from this specialty shop in Pasadena. So Morgan drove all the way there to buy me a dozen. It was really thoughtful. It made me so happy. I ate three and put the rest in the fridge so I could savor them over a few days, but the next morning they were gone. He stayed up late watching a movie and he ate the rest of them. I made this big deal about it because I guess that's what I do with candy. It became this whole stupid thing."

Lilly turns her head to look at her sister. "That's not stupid. It was shitty of him to eat them all."

"But he's the one who bought them to begin with."

"For you. He claimed he bought them for you and then you were supposed

43

to be grateful he got them but ate them? It'd be better if he hadn't gotten them at all."

"Yeah," April feels an uncomfortable stir in her chest. She waits to speak until she knows she can do so without emotion in her voice. "Thank you for saying that. I always thought I overreacted."

Lilly pats her little sister's hand. "Did you fight a lot?"

"No. We hardly ever fought. That candy incident was one of the biggest fights we ever had. I always assumed it was a good thing we didn't argue. I guess I'm just not a fighter," April says.

Lilly gives her sister a look that says, "Since when?" But she catches herself and puts on a blank expression.

Too late. April already saw it. "Yes, you and I fought a lot as kids. I'm not that person anymore."

"Okay," says Lilly, which only annoys April more. She has to stop herself from arguing with Lilly. Otherwise, she'll prove her sister's point.

Maybe she is a fighter.

April climbs out of bed and heads to the kitchen. "I'm gonna get some water."

In the kitchen, April opens the fridge and stares inside, looking for something to soothe her restlessness. The only thing in there is a gallon of two percent milk.

8

Closed Door Sessions

Lilly and April have breakfast before Lilly heads out, leaving her sister with another prolonged hug and an even longer sigh.

April isn't used to being up this early. There's a lot she should be doing at home, so she heads to the library instead. She checks out several books; two books on self-improvement and one on writing. There's nothing quite like procrastinating by going to the library to borrow books on how to beat procrastination.

On her way out the library door, she hears laughter coming from the community room off the lobby. She peeks in to see a crowd of about twenty people facing a series of tables at the front of the room. Several people in business-casual attire sit at the tables while one man, in a fitted dark gray suit, stands at a microphone. He looks out of place with his long hair slicked back behind his ears and his monochromatic runway attire, but his confidence makes him seem right at home. He's smiling. The audience is smiling back.

He's gorgeous and, even though it's been years since she's seen them, April recognizes those brown eyes framed by long, perfectly curved lashes. This is Evan Treks, the first boy to speak to her on her very first day of school in Cleo. She did not imagine how cute he was in eighth grade, because he's just as cute now—probably better.

April takes a seat in the last row and tries to gather what's happening at this meeting. Evan gives some kind of update on a business project for the city while his audience eats up every word he says. Or perhaps that's just April eating his words.

Admittedly, she finds it difficult to concentrate on what he's saying because he's so pretty. He finishes speaking and takes a seat. When he catches April staring at him, she feigns an intense interest in the woman now standing at the microphone. When April dares to glance in Evan's direction, he's watching her with a lovely smile on his lovely face.

After an agonizing few minutes, the meeting ends. Evan makes a beeline for April.

"I heard you'd moved back." He extends his hand and April regrets she's going to have to put her clammy hand in his. Her heart is racing too. It's like she hasn't aged a day over her first day of middle school.

"Evan, I feel like I should know your title. Are you king of Cleo?"

"Oh, just a city commissioner. I still run the investment office. I tried to crown myself king, but it turns out it doesn't work that way."

Evan's family owned a successful investment firm thirty years ago. April guesses by his response that Evan has taken over the business. She nods and smiles. He reaches up with his left hand and gently touches her ball-sacked eye.

Shit. She'd forgotten. Her concealer covers it enough for passersby, but anyone giving her the kind of direct eye contact Evan dishes out right now is sure to notice her shiner.

"Did Coach do this to you?" he asks.

Shit. She'd forgotten about this, too. Nothing stays private in Cleo.

"Well, that didn't take long," she responds.

"Helluva way to announce your arrival." Evan grins from ear to ear, but the only thing annoying about it is his perfect set of teeth. He's still holding her hand and April wishes he'd give it back so she can try to concentrate on anything but him.

An attractive woman approaches and taps Evan on the shoulder to get his attention. "They need you in the closed-door session," she says.

"I'll be right there," he assures her. The woman spares a glance toward April before she leaves as quickly as her pencil skirt and heels will let her.

Evan turns his attention back to Cleo's newest resident.

"She's very serious about her closed-door sessions," April says before really thinking that line through.

Evan's smooth facade glitches for a moment. "That's Alice. She works in the city manager's office." He suddenly remembers that a first name is too intimate for a professional relationship. "Alice Deeds," he adds.

April opens her mouth to apologize for the joke or explain the joke . . . she's not sure which, but a truncated, "Okay," is all that emerges from her throat.

The tremblings of a devious smile perk up the corners of Evan's mouth. The wall of confidence returns. "It's good to have you back, Townsend," he says as he brings his other hand up to encapsulate April's clammy fingers in both his big, warm hands. He somehow looks her even straighter in the eyes.

Townsend. He used to call her that during kickball Fridays in PE. There were two Aprils in the class, so Evan always called this April by her last name to distinguish between the two. At the time, it sent a thrill through her, like a pet name. It still does.

And that eye contact doesn't hurt either. But April tries to hold on to Evan's reaction to the accidental innuendo about Alice, Alice Deeds. That reaction from him suggested the joke hit close to home.

The first month after April and Morgan separated, she experienced online dating for the first time. It was wonderful and horrifying. She got her first unsolicited dick pics (that was part of the horror.) And she decided if she ever wrote another sentence about romance, it would start like this:

Once upon a time, there was no woman in the world who wanted a picture of a stranger's dick. So men began sending pictures of their privates unprovoked, hoping one day, some woman would go, "You know, I didn't ask for this, but now that I have a picture of this stranger's penis, I am suddenly interested in going on a date with this dick."

She also learned the hard way (pun intended) what "ghosting" means. She spent hours texting with men who never intended to meet her—probably because they weren't exactly what they said on their profile. Of course, neither was she. She went by April Eliot, a nod to the nom de plume of author Mary Anne Evans. She couldn't use her maiden name of Townsend, since she used that one to write her book. And she would not use Morgan's last name post-divorce.

So she was April Eliot. A nobody anybody would know.

One positive that came from internet dating was April's discovery that dating without looking for "the one" felt liberating. Of course, she mostly just chatted with men (or people who claimed to be men) online. Meeting a stranger for a date was too scary, both for safety reasons and out-of-practice reasons.

She did sleep with one guy, an acquaintance. When they'd met years ago at an event in L.A., they shared a mutual attraction, but they were both married, so nothing happened. She knew from social media posts he'd gone through a divorce, too. She messaged him; they caught up on the state of their lives. Then they met for drinks and April spent the night at his apartment in Burbank. It was a good night, but April wasn't in any hurry to repeat it.

She realized dating other men would not fix what broke in her the day her husband told her he wanted a divorce. It wasn't just that her heart was broken, it was the embarrassment on a world stage. Her claim to fame was writing a book about finding her true love, but now it turns out she didn't find true love. It turns out she doesn't know any more about love than any other human scrolling through dating apps lying about who they are—maybe even to themselves.

That's when she found Dr. Novacheck, and a lawyer to begin the official divorce process. True to form, Morgan left the work up to her. He told her he wanted the divorce and then he waited for her to make it happen.

In this uninvited phase of her life, she made an effort to focus on the benefits of being single, like the freedom to leave dishes in the sink and avoid arguments about it. Like spending money without consulting anyone. Like selling everything and moving to a small town in Texas without having to explain that decision.

And she promised herself one thing; when she dates again, she is going to acknowledge all the red flags of the men she meets. No justifying, no overlooking, no avoiding questions because she doesn't want to hear the answer, no wishing the red flags away, and no holding on to the myth of a first impression even after it's debunked.

Love does not solve problems. She understands that now much better than she did when she wrote the book about it.

April is determined to let people reveal themselves and to accept what they reveal. She will give her next relationship the courtesy she did not give her first. She will watch it unfold in real time with curiosity instead of fantasy. She will walk into her next romance with her eyes open and her expectations realistic.

At least, that was her plan before running into Evan. This man makes her flutter in ways and in places that make it hard for her to remember her own name, much less her new dating code of conduct.

9

Coffee. Black.

Post black eye debacle, April avoids Daniel. It's been almost a week. When she walked downtown on Monday, she walked on the opposite side of the street from Antic Witties. She scanned the library before entering on Tuesday (to return the books she read cover to cover to avoid doing anything else) because Demmy mentioned Daniel is part of their book club that meets at the library sometimes.

Side note: April absolutely did not go to the library hoping to run into Evan again. The thought didn't even occur to her . . . more than a few times.

She stayed home all day Wednesday and unpacked her entire bedroom, which, yes, okay, consisted of only one box (aside from the dresser box—which went untouched). But progress is progress. And today, Thursday, she's waited to go into Tea'd Off until late afternoon—well after lunch break time.

The bruise around her eye is now easy to cover with a little makeup and her thick rimmed black glasses. Still, she doesn't want Daniel to see the remnants of their first meeting or remember any of the "not appropriate things to say to a man you just met even if you think he's married to another man" things she said at their first meeting.

It's a strange experience to meet someone under such an intimate and embarrassing circumstance. She hasn't gotten over the fact she doesn't know anything about the guy and he's already been in her bedroom . . . and heard her happy ending jokes. It's like jumping the shark of the normal course of getting to know someone.

She will, of course, run into him again. That's how small towns work. But she hopes to at least avoid him until her shiner disappears.

April scans the tables as she enters Tea'd Off. No one she knows is around and there's no one in line as she approaches the counter. She would normally get her drink to go, but she needs to use the Wi-Fi for some document signing on her laptop.

A nonprofit in Atlanta has hired April to teach a story-telling workshop online. She doesn't technically have a literary agent anymore, but a former assistant to her agent recommended her for the job. The pay isn't bad, and the job doesn't involve talking about her story but helping other people tell their stories. April might be a little excited to give it a try. Of course, she's offsetting that excitement with a heaping dose of "this may suck like everything else in my life at the moment".

As soon as she orders her tea at the counter, the door chimes. April looks up to see a woman with a stroller entering as someone holds the door open for her.

Shit. It's Daniel. Daniel holds the door.

Dammit.

She rushes to take a seat in the back of the shop, hoping Daniel will get his plain black coffee or whatever kind of drink he gets (April has this theory nice people order plain black coffee, not because they like it, but because it causes the maker the least amount of trouble) and head back out the front.

She sits on a couch under a painting depicting a giant to-go coffee cup with feet and hands. It holds a briefcase while walking down a sidewalk full of people.

April tries to look busy on her laptop as she sees Daniel approaching in her peripheral vision.

"Hi," he says.

April feigns surprise. "Oh, hi. I didn't see you come in."

A flash of something crosses Daniel's expression before he offers a knowing smile.

"What?" April asks defensively.

Daniel studies her face but says nothing about the remnants of the accident around her eye. "I'm sure you saw me come in," he answers.

April looks up at him over the top frame of her glasses. "Didn't your mother ever tell you it's rude to point out when someone is lying?"

"Can I sit for a minute?" he asks.

"Oh, I'm not staying," April begins. Why does she bother? She's a terrible liar. "Sorry. That doesn't even sound convincing to me."

Daniel seems neither offended nor deterred. "I only need a minute." He sets the timer on his phone to prove it and shows the screen to April.

"Okay, sure," April points to the chair opposite of her. "Listen," she begins as she tries to figure out a way to explain she's not really the woman who way over shared and then knocked herself out by running into a statue. Well . . . she is that woman, but not usually in front of men who are interested in women. Only gay men get the pleasure of hearing her every freaking thought. Actually, now that she thinks about it, it's a wonder she has so many gay friends. Perhaps they're all just being nice.

Daniel is staring at her . . . eyebrows raised . . . waiting.

Shit.

"What were we talking about?" she has to ask.

"You said, 'Listen'. And so I was trying to."

"Yes, well, good job." She falls silent—still unsure how to explain herself.

"Is it okay if I talk now?" Daniel asks. "I only have twenty seconds left." He points to his timer.

"Go for it."

"I'm not interested in dating you," he says in a very matter-of-fact manner. Ouch. April marvels a bit at the sting of that revelation, considering that she's the one who has been avoiding him. "I know there's probably some gentler way to put that, but I'm pretty sure you feel the same and I'm out of time."

The timer on Daniel's phone beeps. He taps it off.

"Go on," says April.

"You're smart. You're funny. I like those qualities in a friend. You're attractive, but I'm willing to overlook that for the sake of our friendship. I think we'd have fun hanging out together if we could skip the weird, nebulous 'what does the other person want from me' phase of our relationship."

Hmmm. So Daniel actually wants to jump the shark—just in the opposite direction.

"Relationship?" April qualifies.

"Not a romantic relationship. But I'm trying to avoid saying 'we're just friends', because it's cliche and also implies that friendship is the consolation prize. I think friendship is, you know, a very excellent prize," he smiles. "Dare I even say, a first prize?"

"I wouldn't," says April. "Sounds too earnest."

"Ok," nods Daniel. "Here's my most unearnest attempt to communicate. I'm not interested in dating you, but I am interested in your company."

"Why?" asks April.

"Because you seem like good company."

"No. Why aren't you interested in dating me?"

"Uh, this feels like a trick question. And my minute is up." Daniel picks up his phone.

"It's not a trick question," says April.

It is a trick question. And Daniel is smart enough to avoid it by asking his own question, "Are you interested in dating me? Is that why you parked on my side of the street Monday, crossed to the opposite side to avoid walking directly in front of my place of employment, and then came back to my side to go into the gift shop right next door to the store where I work?"

April's face burns. "You're very stalkery for someone who claims to want to be just friends."

"You don't have to avoid me. Or, I hope you won't avoid me. That's all I'm saying. You can walk by my storefront. You can say 'hi' when we pass each other in a restaurant. You can even ask me for help with things like putting together the dresser you have in a box in your bedroom, which has been haunting me ever since I saw it." Daniel raises his right hand like he's being sworn in. "I will not put the dresser together and then make an awkward pass at you. I won't hug you for uncomfortably long periods of time when I drink too much. Unless, of course, you request an awkward hug. And, to be fair, I even give those to my male friends if I've been drinking bourbon. So, to fit in as my friend, you may want a sloppy embrace at some point, but until that time, I'm not giving you one because you are my potential friend and I respect your boundaries."

April nods. "Anything else you won't do?"

"I won't hold your hand between mine for an uncomfortably long period of time after a commissioner's meeting."

April absorbs this information. "You saw that?"

"I see a lot of things around here. I try to not talk out of turn, but when my friends have questions, I answer honestly."

"Evan?" She takes his bait.

He nods. "What's your question?"

April isn't sure she wants to know the truth about Evan. Not yet, anyway. So she asks Daniel again, "Why don't you want to date me?"

She's trapped him. He sucks in a breath, like this is not the question he wants to answer. "I'm not manipulating you, if that's what you're asking. I like you. I like your company. I think you're funny."

"But . . . " April prompts.

Daniel carefully considers his words. "You just got divorced. There's a lot to figure out. I know from personal experience. I don't want to distract you from . . ." he struggles to find wording that's not condescending, "what you have to do."

April reads between the lines. She's a mess and he doesn't want to get messy. She moves her eyes from Daniel's face to his cup. His coffee cup.

She pulls down the cardboard sleeve to read his order. Two shots of espresso with a splash of two percent milk. Daniel is full of surprises.

"I'm sorry," she responds, as she slides the cup sleeve back in place. "I didn't hear anything after you said I'm funny. I've been trying desperately to think of a joke about friendship."

Daniel's smile engages the laugh lines around his eyes. He picks up his double espresso from the table and stands. "Think about it. You could text me sometime in a very platonic way." And, with that, he starts to exit.

April calls after him, "What does one friend say to the other as they pass in the ocean?"

Daniel turns back to April. "I don't know."

"We're like two friendships passing in the night."

"You should be a writer," Daniel calls over his shoulder.

"Yeah," she says to herself, "I should."

April sips her tea and sits with her ego. She showed Daniel too much at that first meeting. She was vulnerable, talking about her insecurities. And she needed his help. She accepted his help. As if that wasn't embarrassing enough, he felt like he had to set a boundary with her.

Gross. Gross. No. She is not like that. She is not a mess. She is not someone who gives so much information to total strangers that the stranger has to be like, "Hey, you can stop avoiding me now. I'm not really interested in you enough for you to be embarrassed about the way you behaved."

But you can't say that to someone. You can't prove you're not a mess by going into someone's place of business to say, "By the way, I totally have my shit together, and the last time I interrupted your work day was out of character for me," as you interrupt their work day with your mess.

You know what? Screw that guy. Acting like he's doing her a favor by announcing he doesn't want her romantically and then suggesting she's been avoiding him because she humiliated herself at their first encounter.

She did, of course, humiliate herself. And she was, of course, avoiding him. But a nice guy, a truly nice guy, would have the decency to not address either situation. A good guy would act like he didn't see her walking all the way around the block to avoid his storefront.

April is not a mess. She's . . . a little lost.

She hurts. So much. As far as she has come since her split with Morgan, even moving across the country, it still isn't far enough from the pain of losing her marriage—or losing the dream of her marriage, at least. She didn't ask to be alone in this life. And no matter what she fills her hours with, it doesn't seem to fill the void in her stomach.

Her new "friend" seems to recognize that April has absolutely no idea what she's doing, and he doesn't have the decency to pretend otherwise.

55

10

The Deets

At an Antic Witties open house, Daniel catches April mid-cheese and cracker bite.

"You showed up."

"You invited me."

"Awkward hug?" he offers.

"We're not there yet," she counters.

"No, probably not. I tend to rush into friendships. It scares some people off."

April takes a sip of the mimosa in her hand. "Quick question," she says, "how much of our friendship are you planning to spend talking about our friendship?"

"Like what percentage?"

"Sure."

"Twenty percent." He says it definitively. "Is that too much?"

"Yes."

"Got it. No more talking about our . . ." he points to April and then himself, "but I noticed you walk on this side of the street this week. That's gotta mean something."

April's skin flashes with heat. "Okay. I did some embarrassing shit when we first met and you saw me do it. And you don't want to date me. You've laid it all out there. Can we move forward?"

Daniel holds April's stare with his own. "I'm annoying you."

The way Daniel gets right to the meat and potatoes of a conversation and skips the drinks and appetizers portion of communicating unnerves April. Sometimes she just needs some surface chatting about the weather and sports—and she doesn't even follow any sports.

This is the second time, since the friendly encounter at Tea'd Off, April and Daniel have seen each other. April planned to never purposefully encounter the man again, but she saw him at the library last week while she was not looking for Evan. She got sucked into his and Demmy's book club meeting.

After hearing Daniel's thoughts on the novel they were discussing, April wanted to suggest a book he might enjoy. Of course, she couldn't remember the title. She promised to text him a picture of the cover when she got home.

She found the book in the third box she dug through, right under her first print of *Great Expectations* (not the Dickens' classic but her own poorly titled book on finding love). She took her book and put it in a cabinet so high in the laundry room that she couldn't reach it without a step stool. Then she trudged her ass upstairs (this guy better really appreciate the book suggestion) to retrieve Daniel's business card from the now dusty bureau box. She texted him the book title as promised.

He texted her the next morning to say he enjoyed the book. He read it in one night.

And that was the end of that.

Until this morning, when he texted April an invite to an open house at Antic Witties. She received the text at the precise moment she sat down to put her bureau together. The timing was perfect. When procrastination calls (or texts), April answers.

Now that she's here talking to Daniel once again about their friendship, she's annoyed by him and he is aware she's annoyed. She's not sorry she came. She got to chat with Demmy for a bit. Plus, the snack table is on point and the mimosas are free. But now, she needs an excuse to leave.

Jayda Nelson interrupts their conversation, and even Daniel is going to break from his interrogation of April to answer a question from a customer.

"Daniel darling," says Jayda with her charming Texas drawl, "how much is that armoire in the corner?"

"For you? Five hundred and I'll deliver it for free." Daniel turns his full attention to Jayda, allowing April to slip out of his line of fire. She walks away from the charcuterie board (which is difficult to do) and heads toward the front door. Behind her, she hears Daniel say, "Jayda, how is Howard doing?"

Jayda's voice trails off. "You are so sweet for asking . . ."

April steps outside, glancing in each direction to calculate her next move. She made a step toward an amicable acquaintanceship, if not a friendship, with Daniel. Now she'd like to move on.

To her right, Evan appears like an angel swooping in for a save. He wears a blue suit that fits him perfectly. He smiles the moment April locks eyes with him and any ounce of annoyance she has for Daniel retreats, along with her willpower.

Jeez, she says to herself. *Get your shit together.* It's just been so many years since someone made her react like this. Every part of her switches to high alert when Evan is in range.

He has a fucking man-bun. You hate men with buns, she thinks. But her body isn't getting the message.

Her breath catches as she attempts to let out a confident, "Hello." She chokes on her own spit.

"You ok?" Evan's hand lands with concern on April's back and she pulls away from the jolt his touch sends through her.

He steps back. "Sorry."

"No, I'm . . . no, you're fine. I mean, your touching me is fine. You did nothing wrong, is what I'm saying. I'm . . . honestly, I'm just flustered."

"What happened?"

"You." She gives up trying to pretend to have it together around him. "You happened."

Evan enjoys this. "I fluster you? The great author April Townsend?"

"You are aware of the power you have over women."

"Are you a woman?" Evan acts surprised. "I hadn't noticed. I mean, the first day we met at the library, you wore that green dress that matched your eyes and the strap kept slipping off your left shoulder while you sat in on the council meeting. I guess I noticed that." He holds her stare for a moment. She can't help grinning while she shakes her head.

"What?" he asks.

"I need to stay away from you," she answers.

"I'm harmless."

"Does your girlfriend think so?"

"What girlfriend?"

"The one who enjoys closed-door sessions," April says.

"Alice is not my girlfriend," Evan replies.

"Does she know that?"

Evan looks suddenly serious as his right hand gently grabs the fingertips of April's left hand. He leans in closer and whispers, "I don't have a girlfriend. All of them know that."

April laughs even though there's probably a lot of truth in Evan's joke. He gestures toward the shop door behind them. "I need to go in there and be seen. Will you join me?" He offers his arm to her, but she declines.

"I'm still new in town. I can't risk pissing off all the ladies yet."

Evan takes one step toward the door and turns back. "There's an art event next Saturday, Townsend. You gonna be there?"

"I don't know anything about it."

"I'll text you the deets," he says with a hell of an inviting smile. A smile so inviting, in fact, it makes one overlook the fact that he used the term "deets".

"Are you asking for my number?" April replies.

"Don't need to," Evan says with confidence. "I'll text you."

He turns toward the door again and jumps at the unexpected body of Daniel exiting the shop, just as Evan flirts his way in.

"Oh, excuse me," says Evan. When Daniel is past him, Evan turns and makes a face behind his back like "whoops". He shrugs and disappears inside.

Daniel fills his lungs with the cool fall air. He shoves his hands in his pockets. "It's crowded in there," he says.

"That's good, right?" says April.

"Yes. Yeah. That's good. Look, I'm sorry if I've made things uncomfortable between us."

"No," April starts to protest, but then remembers what it feels like to have someone deny what you know to be true. Daniel is straightforward with her, maybe too straightforward. She'll give him the same.

"I'm not used to your directness."

Daniel looks thoughtful. "What's your preferred approach to honesty?"

"Uh . . . avoidance, like every other normal human being."

"You didn't have any issue with directness when we met. The first thing you talked to me about was re-homing your mattresses after your divorce."

"I never mentioned my divorce," April corrects him. "You inferred that part. That's what's weird for me, everyone can easily look up very personal things about my life. Like, that I'm recently divorced and don't need distractions from doing whatever it is I have to do."

Daniel recognizes his own words he used against April when they met in Tea'd Off. He also recognizes his mistake.

"I'm sorry," he groans. "I'm an idiot. You're right. That's not fair at all."

April shrugs. "I mean, I did write a very personal book. That's my own fault. Anyone who has read it feels like they know me."

"Well . . ." Daniel says, "I didn't read your book yet. I just liked that in our first conversation we got right to something interesting."

April isn't sure whether she's glad or offended Daniel hasn't read her work. The man can read a book in one night, he doesn't really have the excuse of time. "Yeah, well," she decides to just lay the truth out there, "I thought you were married to Joel when we first met."

Daniel's expression is blank. "No. I'm not married to my brother."

"I didn't realize Joel was your brother. He was talking about his husband and then he said you, Daniel, run the store. And I inferred the rest."

Daniel doesn't even try to control the shit-eating grin on his face. "So how would our conversation have gone if you didn't believe I was married to my brother?"

"Uh, it would have been much less interesting," April acknowledges.

"That's too bad. I liked that conversation. It had some depth to it."

"It was about happy endings," April says with zero inflection.

Daniel comes to the defense of their initial exchange. "It was about inanimate objects carrying our stories versus having a life of their own. I've been thinking about that concept ever since."

"Alright, well," April sighs, "at least warm me up a little bit. I can't just jump into a meaningful conversation with you now that I'm aware you're . . ."

Daniel finishes her sentence, "not married to my brother".

"I mean, we barely know each other," April continues. "At least mention the weather before you tell me how you feel about my unhealthy obsession with avoiding pain and my complicated relationship with my father."

Daniel considers this before he responds, "I read today it's supposed to rain in the next month. How do you think your father would feel about that?"

April doesn't get to complete her eye roll before Daniel continues, "I get it," he says as he puts his hand on her shoulder. "I tend to jump right in. Small talk is not my foreplay, but if you need a warm-up, I can make that happen."

April can't believe what she just heard. Her mouth falls open. "I thought we were just friends."

Daniel's eyes narrow. "So did I."

"Friends don't flirt with each other that way."

"What way?" Daniel asks as he removes his hand from her shoulder.

"You know what you said." April stands taller. She will not play this game where a guy embarrasses her for having such a *dirty mind* when he merely made an innocent statement.

Daniel takes a small step back. "April, I know what I said, but I think I need to know what you think I said."

Based off the look on Daniel's face, April is suddenly very unsure of herself. "You said small talk is not your foreplay." The truth hits April as soon as she says it. "Oh my god, you said 'forte' didn't you?"

"Yes. I said small talk is not my forte. I swear." Daniel's words sound sincere, but he's smiling—whether from amusement or discomfort April can't tell. No wonder she couldn't believe what she heard, because she hadn't actually fucking heard it! Because "foreplay" makes zero sense and "forte" makes all the sense.

Daniel stops smiling when he sees the color of April's cheeks. "Oh no! Don't be . . ."

"Embarrassed?" April finishes. "What is it about you that makes me keep making a fool of myself?"

"Listen," Daniel says seriously, "small talk really is not my forte. Apparently, neither is big talk." He points toward Tea'd Off down the street. "Announcing I want to be friends? Who does that?! And 'forte'?! No one uses that word. That's a dumb fucking word."

April appreciates his efforts.

"Now, foreplay," he continues, "that's a great word, and, you know, general concept. Very important concept. No wonder you heard that word, because it's a much better choice than the one I made. That's why you're a writer and I'm just a guy running an antique shop."

"Can we pretend this conversation never happened and start again the next time we run into each other?" April pleads.

"Only if we can also forget the conversation in Tea'd Off," Daniel adds.

"I wouldn't mind forgetting the black eye incident," April says.

"You know what?" says Daniel. "Next time we meet, we start all over. I'm even going to forget about the book you recommended. I've never read or enjoyed reading it. Can we start fresh?" He offers his hand and April shakes it in agreement.

"Great," says Daniel as he heads back inside his business. Then he turns for a quick aside to April, "But recommend that book to me again, because I liked it."

"'Til next time, Stranger," says April as she does a two-finger salute toward Daniel and immediately regrets it. Why can't she control herself around this guy?

11

Cow

When I first moved to L.A., I worked as a receptionist in a building for entertainment types; lawyers, agents, producers, etc. I sat at a large, circular desk in the middle of a grand lobby in a high-rise on Wilshire. I spent most of the day observing people passing in and out of the glass doors lining the front of the building.

That's where I first noticed this phenomenon of men "guiding" women through doorways by fanning their large hands across the small of a woman's back.

Many times, I watched women stiffen at the uninvited touch, even as a polite smile filled their faces.

Other times, I could practically see the sparks flying, like touching two jumper cables together. I knew who was having an affair with whom before anyone else in the building figured it out. And I knew when an affair ended, because the couple would go through the motions of working together, but the man stopped putting his hand on the woman's back to guide her through doorways. She was left to her own devices to find her way into and out of the building.

Somehow, she always figured it out.

Excerpt from *Great Expectations* by April Townsend

Next time April and Daniel meet, as it turns out, is a week later at the pop-up art gallery in the old Interstate Bank Building. Evan made good on his promise; he texted April without explaining how he got her number. They made plans to meet at the event.

April happily spent the afternoon away from home, working (a.k.a. procrastinating) as a test model for the new cosmetic line at Linda's Boutique. Her eyes are now lined in black liner, winging out and up in the corners. Her lipstick is a bright red. These are two makeup applications she never trusts herself to perform. She wears a high-waisted, fifties-style floral dress (that helps to hide her post-marriage love handles).

As soon as she enters the gallery downtown, she's self-conscious. There are lots of people from the big city with dark colored, flowy clothes and earthy looking shoes. April is like a spotlight in her red heels.

Evan is supposed to meet her here, but she doesn't see him yet. The space is dark except for the glossy finish of the paintings in the gallery spotlights. It's a different energy from most spaces in Cleo. If April didn't know better, she could swear she was in some sexy little artist loft off Laurel Canyon in Hollywood as she grabs a glass of champagne.

From across the room, Anna Gale spots April and motions for her to join the small group gathered around an abstract painting of what appears to be a four-legged animal. April met Anna and her husband, Thomas, at a lunch meeting arranged by Demmy earlier this week. The Gales need board members for their non-profit arts project.

As April approaches, she realizes that Daniel stands between Anna and Thomas. Anna makes a show of kissing April's cheeks while Thomas kisses her hand as a greeting.

"My darling girl," says Anna, "I'm mortified to tell you I didn't get to read your book this week. Thomas insisted we spend the week at our condo in Aspen and I forgot my reading glasses."

"It's no problem," April begins, but is immediately interrupted.

"Look at me!" Anna throws up her hands. "You'd think I've never been out in good society. April, you do know Daniel, don't you?"

April opens her mouth to confirm, but Daniel gets there first. "No, actually. I don't believe I've had the pleasure. I'm Daniel." He reaches his hand out as April's brow furrows in confusion. "We haven't met yet, have we?" he asks.

April catches on. Daniel actually intends to follow through on the agreement they made during their last conversation. They are starting over.

"No, I don't think so," she responds.

A warm smile crosses Daniel's face as April's hand meets his in the middle. He gives her fingers a gentle squeeze. "It's very nice to finally meet you, April," Daniel emphasizes the very.

That smile, and that squeeze and that "very" cause an involuntary moment of confusion in April's belly. Daniel looks good in his dark jeans and boots. He's got glasses April hasn't seen him wear before and a gray corduroy jacket. The look suits him.

In addition, April finds she likes hearing her name on Daniel's lips.

Uh-oh. Thomas is speaking. April tries to catch up to the conversation. Apparently, it's something about being surprised April and Daniel don't already know each other because Daniel responds, "I know who she is, of course. I read her book."

"You did?" April says in surprise.

"Yes, I did."

"What did you think of the book?" asks Anna. "I've heard it's brilliant."

Daniel keeps his attention on April even while he answers Anna. "I think I can't stop thinking about it."

April tries to return Daniel's focus with equal intensity. "That's not always a good thing."

"It is in this case. You know, writing is not my forte. But I can certainly enjoy it when it's done well."

If words can change the temperature of a space, Daniel's words just made the room five degrees warmer. Even April questions whether or not she's met this Daniel before.

She can't keep up the eye contact anymore. It's like playing chicken with another car and she veers away first. She glances down at her champagne glass and attempts to gather her wits.

What is happening here? This feels like some kind of role playing game where fantasy and reality blur, and April's not sure what the rules are, and she's . . . well, honestly, she's just way into it.

Why is this so fun?!

Normally, it would be wrong to have this inside joke between two people in a group of four, but Anna and Thomas are much too involved in their own orbit to have a vested interest in the gravitational pull between April and Daniel.

April attempts to put her attention on Thomas's monologue about meeting one of the artists. But even with her head turned away from Daniel, she can't stop her focus from going to him. It's like the side of her body facing him is in another climate zone from her other half. At one point in the superfluous conversation happening between the Gales, April is certain Daniel has moved within inches of her because she can feel his heat warming the left side of her body, but when she dares to glance at him, he's still a good two feet across from her.

A waiter interrupts April's thoughts to take her empty champagne glass. She's happy to have the spell broken for a moment. Daniel offers to get her another drink from the bar and, though she doesn't plan to drink anymore (her body is already not cooperating), she's glad to have a reason to send him away so she can collect herself.

She still can't focus on Anna's babble as she watches Daniel walk to the bar and admires his . . .

"Hello."

April starts at the voice coming from right behind her.

Evan. Yes. Right. Evan, who she is supposed to meet here, is . . . here.

He smiles that disarming smile (which is aided greatly by the dimple on his left cheek) as he greets April and the others.

"Oh, Evan, dear!" Anna makes a show of kissing him on both cheeks as she does with everyone. Evan matches her fanfare, and April can't quite discern if he's doing so because he enjoys it or because he's making a joke of it.

Other than dropping her drink off, Daniel ignores April for the better part of the gallery opening. Or, at least, he doesn't interact with her. Whether that's on purpose, April can't know.

Evan gives her plenty of attention, which would be very enjoyable had it not been preempted by that five-minute role play of Daniel's. He spoiled her for any other male attention during the event, like getting a couple bites of the most delicious dessert first and then trying to be equally enthusiastic

66

over a decent grilled chicken.

April finds herself constantly aware of Daniel's presence in the room. When she and Evan are visiting with Demmy, Daniel is on the opposite side of the event talking to an attractive couple from Dallas. While Evan introduces April to a young woman just moving back from college, Daniel stands under the exit sign in the far right corner and chats with one of the artists.

Around 11 p.m., Evan goes to close out their tab as April visits with her makeup designer of the evening, THE Linda from Linda's Boutique. Daniel is only a few feet behind April, talking with Demmy and Anna.

It seems to April that she and Daniel are pulling toward each other like magnets. When Linda wanders off, April turns around to discover Daniel isn't there at all. She's feeling phantom Daniels in this room. He's haunting her.

All evening she has tried to be present, but it's like her body is a heat-seeking missile and Daniel is the . . . well, he's the heat.

Eighth grade April is asking adult April what the hell is wrong with her. Evan Treks, wearing his cashmere v-neck sweater with his perfectly perfect slacks (which look like someone sewed them on him) and that dimple thirteen-year-old April dreamed about touching, is pouring attention over mid-forties April. But she's letting herself get distracted by the guy wearing cowboy boots who only wants to be her friend but also just role played the hell out of . . .

Stop. Stop it, April demands of herself as she stares at the abstract painting closest to her. It's that four-legged beast again.

"What do you think of the cow?" Daniel's deep voice comes from close behind April. The hairs on the back of her neck prickle. She stands up straighter to cover the shiver rolling down her spine.

"Is it a cow?" she asks as she tilts her head to look at the painting from a different angle.

Daniel comes to stand on her right side. "It says it's a cow," he points to the title card next to the piece, which reads:

"Cow"

Oil on Canvas

R.D.

$950

Daniel continues, "If it looks like a cow and it says it's a cow, it's probably . . ."

"A friend," April finishes his sentence. "It's probably just a friend."

April feels Daniel turn to her—a concerned look on his face, just as Evan saddles up to her left and drapes his arm over her shoulder.

"Hay!" he says.

To which April replies, "Hey!"

"No," says Evan as he points to the round bail painted behind the cow's ass. "Hay."

"Oh," April replies with a half-assed laugh. She takes a breath in and turns to address Daniel, but he mercifully beats her to the punch.

"Well, I'm headed home," Daniel begins. Before he can finish his sentence, Evan interrupts.

"Us too," says Evan, and April winces at the wording. They aren't headed home together, but she stops herself from over explaining. The three head toward the exit, with Evan and Daniel chatting about a mutual acquaintance.

As they leave the building, Evan holds the door open with one hand and puts his other hand on the small of April's back to guide her through the doorway. April glances behind her, hoping Daniel didn't see the gesture. No such luck. He catches her eye and shares a knowing expression.

He did read her book.

"Goodnight," says Daniel as he moves away from Evan and April in the parking lot.

"Goodnight," say Evan and April at exactly the same moment, making April cringe a bit.

Evan has his hands in his pockets as they arrive at April's car. She unlocks the door and turns to face him as he finishes a funny story about a constituent calling to complain about the state of the roads and then asking Evan for his barbecue recipe.

It's impossible to dislike Evan. He's charming, even when he knows he's being charming. He offers his hand to April. When she takes it, he wraps her hand in both of his just like he did at the library. He focuses all his attention on April and she beams up at him. She can't help it. Evan is a light and when he's shining on someone, they light up too. No wonder this guy is in politics. He could charm the skin off a snake.

"Thank you for a fun night," he says sincerely as he kisses April on the cheek. Over Evan's shoulder, April spots Daniel glancing her way as he keys into his truck. April does not want Daniel seeing Evan kiss her, but Daniel gives a small wave of acknowledgment—as though nothing is amiss. Suddenly, April realizes Daniel is whispering something in her ear. Wait, no. Evan . . . Evan is whispering something.

April shakes her head as though that will straighten out her thoughts. Evan believes she's shaking her head in response to his whispers. He pulls back to look at her, still holding her hand in both of his.

"No?" he asks.

"No. I mean, not no," she responds.

"So yes?" he asks hopefully.

"No," she laughs. How does a woman explain that she was just trying to shake off thinking the guy whispering to her was another guy. "I didn't hear you. What did you say?"

Evan hesitates. He tries to read April's expression, as though she's playing at something he can't quite figure out. His lips press into a confident smile. "It's not important," he says as he reaches behind April to open her car door. "Good night, Townsend."

12

Largemouth Bass

"So," Demmy doesn't even try to segue gracefully to the subject she's most interested in. "Did you have fun at the pop-up gallery?"

"Yes," April says. But Demmy isn't buying it. She stares until April is unsure of the correct answer. "It was fun?"

"I know you're an adult. I know you can decide for yourself. But it has been a long time since you lived in a small town, dated in a small town. I feel it's my duty to remind you it's not like the big city here. There's a reason dogs don't pee where they eat. You know what I'm saying?"

"No. But thank you for the visual."

Demmy sighs as she steps onto a ladder to hang a handmade sign that reads, *You Got This.* Demmy has volunteered herself and April to work on the displays for the "Crafts for Kids" event at the community center. Businesses all over town create something to be auctioned off and 'the funds raised go to providing holiday meals and toys for kids in Cleo. The other volunteers today are members of Mrs. Turner's second grade class at Cleo Elementary.

"I'm just saying this isn't like Los Angeles," Demmy continues. "You sleep with someone here and then you have to see them at church on Sunday." Demmy looks down from the third step on the ladder to see two of Mrs. Turner's boys gaping up at her, their eyes wide.

The littlest one says, "My mom tells me to have my friend Mark sleep over on Saturdays so he can go to church with us Sunday morning. His mama doesn't take him to church otherwise because she's a hippie."

"I'm not sure I'd tell anyone else that story, Troy," Demmy says flatly. "Go get a brownie from the kitchen." She finishes hanging the glitter covered sign and steps back down to April's level. "You understand what I mean about dating men here." It's not a question.

April smiles. "Don't worry. There's no risk of me running into a guy at church that I've slept with. I don't even go to church."

Demmy isn't amused. "That's only part of your problem. Listen, take it from someone who hears everything around here. It's not like you have time in Cleo to experiment with a guy, test the waters and then head to the beach. You're in the same water, and so are your neighbor, your coworker and your postman. You have to be pretty da…", Demmy remembers where she is, "darn sure you want what you're fishing for. Otherwise, it's not worth the gossip, or having to avoid your favorite restaurants because your largemouth bass goes there too."

Judging by Demmy's vehemence, April guesses the woman speaks from experience. Still, she can't take this conversation too seriously when Demmy is making fish metaphors. "What makes Evan a largemouth bass?" April whispers.

Demmy's brow furrows. "I'm not worried about Evan. That man knows how to cut bait and run."

"Look," says April as she pats her friend's shoulder, "you don't need to worry about me."

Demmy glares at April's hand where it touches her. "I'm not worried about you either."

April pulls her hand back in disgust. "Then I take back that reassuring shoulder pat."

"You can't take back a gesture you already performed. That's my whole point."

Children are now wandering into the room. Demmy chooses her words carefully. "Once you do something to somebody, it is done. You patted me and now you are gonna have to run into me Thursday at the Rotary lunch.

You're gonna run into me Wednesday at Tea'd Off. And you're gonna run into me later today when you come over to my house to help me finish the goody bags for the auction. Now, that may be fine for you, but you have to consider my feelings too. That pat might mean a lot more to me than it means to you."

"Demmy, how long has it been since you've been with someone?" April asks. "Because a shoulder pat is very innocent. That's like not even first base. That's not even on the field. It's in the bleachers or maybe even the parking lot."

"You joke, but I'm serious." Demmy's eyes shift to the doorway. "Speak of the devil."

April follows Demmy's gaze to see Daniel walking into the event center with what looks like a TV box in his arms. She turns back to her friend in surprise.

"You're worried I'll catch and release Daniel?"

"You're gonna try to act surprised?"

"I am surprised. I never talked to you about Daniel."

Demmy loses her patience. "I've got eyes. I'm just saying, he's a really good guy. Be careful with him."

April starts to object, but she's interrupted by a, "Hello." She jumps at the sound of Daniel so close behind her.

"Sorry, didn't mean to sneak up on you," he apologizes.

"Mmm hmm," hums Demmy.

"That's okay," says April. "We were just talking about fishing."

"Oh, do you fish?" Daniel asks.

Both ladies answer, "No."

Daniel nods. "So I didn't interrupt much."

"No," says Demmy, "The conversation was over before it began."

"As are all good conversations," says April.

Daniel looks between the ladies. "Well, this is uncomfortable . . . goodbye." He turns to leave and calls over his shoulder, "I left the sign on the stage."

"Thank you, Daniel," calls Demmy. He throws his hand up in a wave and leaves as quickly as he came in.

Demmy turns her attention to April. "What?" April protests. "Surely you didn't read anything into that. He barely looked at me."

"Because you were weird," Demmy laughs.

"You're the one who said you're worried about the man interacting with me. If I make every interaction weird, he won't try to take my bait," April raises her eyebrows on the last part to suggest something rated R.

Demmy acts annoyed, but she's smiling, "You're disgusting."

"You're the one who called him a largemouth bass!" April protests.

"I'm telling you he's one of the good ones, and I'm asking you to avoid starting something unless you know you want to finish it. That's all."

April is at least slightly offended Demmy keeps reiterating what a good guy Daniel is, as though that's a warning sign for April to stay away—as though April could somehow ruin his good guyness. April recalls the role playing game Daniel led at the gallery. (She might actually be recalling it too much and too often.) He wasn't such a good guy that night. In fact, he was downright bad. That's what made it so hot.

If anything, April should stay away from HIM. Daniel claims he's a friend, but he flirts like a madman at the art reception and then he walks out chatting casually with April's date. Perhaps he's the dangerous one.

"Will you please finish putting out the signs on the stage? There are easels for the larger ones." Demmy grabs her computer bag and checks to be sure she has her keys.

"Yes," says April. "And for the record, Daniel told me explicitly he wants to be friends."

"Good," says Demmy, "I like a man who's honest and upfront."

"I'M honest and upfront," April insists.

"Then you two should be great friends," Demmy says as she heads for the exit. "I'll see you at my house around six. I'll order pizza."

"To be honest and upfront with you, I like pepperoni with easy sauce," April calls after her friend.

Demmy shakes her head as she swings the door open. "Of course you do."

"What's that supposed to mean?" April gets no response.

This is ridiculous. Does Demmy really think Daniel is too good for her?

She's good. Just this morning she flipped a penny over to be face up on the ground so someone else could receive the good luck she couldn't.

April wanders over to the easels laying in a pile at the foot of the stage. She sets two of them up a few feet apart for the two framed signs on the lip of the stage. The other signs she's hung with Demmy today have been much more simple than these. These are more like works of art. They're auctioned off at the end of the night as the finale to the fundraiser.

The first one April displays on an easel is a mixed media piece created by the art department at the local junior college. It's full of quotes about strength.

The second piece is a beautiful portrait of a pond and on the shore is the word "faith" written in small print. The reflection of the word in the ripples of the water is twice the size of the word on the shore. An artist named Andy signed the work, but the card slipped into the corner of the frame reads, *Donated by the Trek Company.* Evan's family must have commissioned the piece. They've always been generous with nonprofits in town.

April rearranges a few of the smaller signs sitting on a table before noticing the box Daniel brought in. She opens the top and slides out the framed art inside.

It's like a cross between a wood sculpture and a painting. The left side of the wood frame is taller than the rest, and it's carved into a tree reaching up and over the top of the piece. Inside the frame is a painting of the woods. There are dozens of trees of all shapes and sizes. Tall and thin. Round and small. Tiny. Towering. Some have autumn leaves. Some have green. Some have bare winter branches with their leaves gathered around them on the ground. There's even a little seedling in the front with barely visible buds. Hidden somewhere in the bark of every tree is the word *growing.* And when April looks at the carved frame, she even finds it etched into the bark on the bottom . . .

Growing.

The piece is light, even with the large wood frame. April holds it while she searches the surface, looking for the artists' signature. There it is, carved into the lower right corner of the frame, the artist's initials.

R.D.

Suddenly, April remembers exactly who Daniel is.

13

Talent

Demmy and April finish the goody bags for the auction. Then, after some delicious pepperoni, easy-sauce pizza, April asks Demmy if she has any of her old yearbooks.

Demmy pulls four of them (from every year of her high school days) off the bookshelf in her living room. April pretends to look through them at random, but what she's really looking for is the photo on page 52 of the yearbook from her freshman year. There is a black-and-white photo of a kid with shaggy hair and baggy clothes working on the set of *Into the Woods*. Below the photo reads the name, Robert Daniel Rayburn.

Demmy catches April staring at the photo for a beat too long. "I knew it," she says.

"What?!"

"Don't even pretend you were looking at those books for anything else but that photo."

April acquiesces, "Alright. I remember him now. But I knew him as Robert."

"I think Mrs. Goodman was the only one who called him that. He usually went by Daniel," says Demmy.

"That tower he built for *Into the Woods* was incredible—especially for a high schooler."

Demmy nods. "He did the whole set. He even built Milky White." Milky White is the name of the cow in *Into the Woods*.

The cow.

Cow.

Cow at the pop up gallery.

Son-of-a-bitch!

"The painting at the pop up !" April is not amused. "Why didn't you tell me? I talked to him about that piece. I must have sounded like an asshole."

"If he wanted you to know, he would have told you himself," Demmy says.

"He probably assumed I already knew!"

"You'd be surprised. A lot of people in town don't realize how much he's done. He also did the mural in the alley behind Antic Witties and the big painting in the back of Tea'd Off."

"The giant coffee too?" April looks skeptical. "So he's like the Banksy of small town Texas? I run into a statue's balls and everyone in town knows about it in two minutes, but this guy creates art all over town and nobody bats an eye?"

"He just doesn't want a big thing, I guess."

"That's dumb. He's trying too hard to be humble. It's like not telling someone it's your birthday when you're hanging out with them on your birthday—makes people feel like assholes when they go home and see on social media that it's your freaking birthday!"

Demmy assumes a neutral tone. "Do you go around telling everyone you wrote a book?"

Demmy makes a point, but April won't admit it. "No, but my book also doesn't hang on a wall in plain sight. He's talented. He should just own it."

"You're talented," Demmy says. It sounds more like a challenge than a compliment.

"YOU'RE talented," April says in an equally challenging manner as she points to a yearbook photo of a teenage Demmy singing in a spotlight.

Demmy stares at her picture. "Where did I get all that confidence?"

"My hand!" April squeals.

"You handed me confidence?" Demmy asks.

"My hand is in the picture." April looks incredulously at Demmy, as though it was very obvious to everyone (even though it's only the two of them in the room) that when April screamed, "My hand!", she was referring to the nearly invisible knuckles holding the stage curtain behind teenage Demmy in the black and photo in the twenty-five-year-old yearbook.

Demmy squints at the tiny portion of a finger in the pic. "How can you tell?"

"Lilly gave me that ring for Valentine's Day."

Demmy squints harder to see a little ring with a little heart on the little ring finger in the picture.

"She gave it to me to cheer me up because she was very aware no one else would be giving me anything." April fills with emotion. She's thankful her phone buzzes with a text. It gives her an excuse to walk over to her purse.

It's from Evan.

Evan: Come over and have a drink. I have something to show you.

April smiles on accident as she reads the text. Demmy is all over it. "Is that a booty call?"

"No!" April says this vehemently, even though it might well be a booty call. "But I do have to go."

April thanks Demmy for dinner and rushes to the safety of her car interior to text Evan back.

April: Yeah, I'm sure you do.

Evan: Not that, Townsend. Get your mind out of the gutter. Only need five minutes.

As April tries to form a response to the five-minute reference, Evan texts again.

Evan: And no, I'm not talking about the bedroom. If I was talking about that, I'd need hours.

April considers how, after a decade of being married to Morgan, hours of sex became unappealing. In general, one grows into their sexual years thinking *"the longer, the better"*. But around year ten for Morgan and April, her mantra was "the *shorter, the sooner I can go to sleep"*.

She tries to imagine whether she'd enjoy hours of sex with Evan. This means, of course, she has to imagine having sex with Evan, which is a very dangerous thought process considering he just texted his address to her. She promises herself she will stop by. That is it. A stop by that doesn't involve nudity or groping. And she knows she'll stick to that pledge because she hasn't shaved in a week. Unshaven is her D.I.Y. chastity belt.

Evan answers the door in his suit pants and button down. His feet are bare, his tie undone. The look is very sexy. Of course, Evan likely curated this exact response. He understands the pull he has. April keeps her distance and refuses the wine he offers. He seems bemused by her efforts to resist his charms.

As they walk down a hallway in his (very nice) house, Evan pauses at a closed door and turns to April. "I'm not going to try anything . . . not until you ask. I really do just want to show you this . . ."

He turns the doorknob and pushes the door open with flare to reveal a cozy study. There's a mahogany desk, bookshelves full of only hardcover books, and a beautifully lit piece of art taking up most of the wall on the opposite side of the room.

April recognizes the art from the pop up gallery. It hung two spots down from Daniel's cow. It's a colorful and modern contrast to the old school feel of the rest of the room.

"I don't recall you looking much at this one," she says.

"It was hard to look at much of anything but you," Evan responds. And, though he sounds serious, April can't take him seriously.

"I'm serious," he insists. "That vintage vibe suits you. You were the most interesting art piece in the room."

"Did you just call me a 'piece'?" she smiles.

"Okay, you were the most interesting work of art in that room."

"So now I'm a piece of work?"

Evan shakes his head as he steps closer to April. "Yes, you are a piece of work."

April studies the artwork in order to turn her attention away from Evan. It's bright and chaotic. There appears to be some type of string emerging in places—like a ball of yarn vomited on the canvas. April's not sure what to make of it.

"What is it about this one that made you want it?" She asks this while

79

taking a tiny step away from Evan so his shoulder doesn't touch her anymore. Before he can answer something charming, she instructs him, "And don't answer that question as though it's about me. I'm talking about the painting."

Evan laughs. He was definitely about to attempt a romantic moment before she cut him off. He faces the painting. "I don't understand it," he answers. April notes that he sounds different; sincere. Maybe for the first time since they've met as adults.

She looks at Evan's profile. Those curled eyelashes greeted her all those years ago in the middle school gym. "Isn't the whole point of buying art to buy something that speaks to you?" she asks.

"I used to think so," Evan says. "This spot on the wall has been empty since I redid the place a year ago. I've looked at hundreds of prints and original pieces and nothing stood out to me. This is the first one I thought about the next day. It's the first one I didn't get right away. And it made me wonder if the point of collecting art is not owning something I already understand, but something I want to figure out."

April can feel the sleeve of Evan's button down very barely tickling her arm as her heartbeat picks up. She shouldn't fall for this heady art/philosophical stuff. She really should not. Fall. For. This. Heady. Stuff . . .

"What's it called?" she asks.

Evan smiles. *The Common Thread.*

April sees it now. The art is a bunch of different things. Like it doesn't even know what it is. It's decoupage with various prints and writings. It's spray paint and some acrylic with no particular pattern. It's plaster that seems arbitrary in some spots and carefully placed in others.

And then there's the effort to make sense of it all—the thin, fragile yarn connecting all the randomness into a brash, loud, confusing piece of art that could be brilliant or could be a half-assed mess.

It's a painting of April's life.

"Do you like it?" asks Evan as his shoulder touches hers.

"I'm not sure," says April. "Maybe."

14

Moving On

April left Evan's house on Thursday night, staying completely true to her word. Nothing happened with Evan. Yes, their pinkies touched. Not a big deal. Yes, they hugged goodbye a beat longer than a normal friend hug should last. Nothing to be ashamed of. And then there was, you know, that kiss . . . on the lips . . . that lingered . . . with lips slightly parted. That probably was not nothing. But, overall, April's stubble did indeed keep her from doing anything she'd regret too much.

And she wakes up this beautiful, fall morning with a big smile and a new sense of motivation. She can do difficult things. She can trust herself. She can have nice kisses with her eighth-grade crush without a twinge of guilt.

She finally unpacks those book boxes and makes some phone calls she's been putting off for weeks. She calls her parents and Lilly, who she hasn't heard from since her visit.

Lilly doesn't answer, which is even better. Now, April made an effort, but doesn't actually have to talk to her sister.

She spends the early afternoon completing her curriculum for the online class she's teaching, and spends the rest of the afternoon running a few errands downtown. She even shaves and throws on a dress.

As April leaves the post office just before it closes, Lilly calls. April lets it go to voicemail—she's already done her duty in calling earlier. But Lilly leaves a cryptic message, so April rolls her eyes as she sits in the parking lot of the post office and calls her sister back.

After the initial exchange of pleasantries, Lilly dives in, "So, I'm glad you called because I've been needing to call you. I just didn't know what to say. I got a text from Morgan."

Instantly, April's biology rewinds eight months. Her body is right back there, sitting at her kitchen counter having coffee and a chocolate chip cookie when she gets a text from her husband. *We've got to talk.*

"About what?" April says to her sister in the present.

"There's no easy way to say this."

"Lilly, get it over with."

"He's seeing someone."

All the progress April has made climbing out of the hole in the pit of her stomach undoes itself. She slips back into the same feelings of despair she had right after the breakup.

The tears are coming. Unwelcome as they are, April can't stop them. She doesn't speak. She can't trust her voice.

Lilly fills the silence. "He wasn't sure if he should reach out to let you know. I told him not to. And I wasn't sure if I should tell you, but Trey thought I should. Maybe it's easier hearing it from me than him?"

"He knew you'd tell me so he wouldn't have to," April says.

"Would you rather he called you himself?"

"He wouldn't have called. He would have texted."

"I'm sorry," Lilly responds. It's unclear if she means about the texting or the fact that April's ex-husband of fourteen years is already dating someone.

"No," says April. "No. I would rather hear it from someone who loves me."

"I do love you," Lilly says.

April can't bring herself to return the reassurance. It would open the floodgates. Instead, she says, "I guess it's serious if he thought I should know about it."

"I think so." Lilly's voice is small. She sounds like the girl who let her little sister sleep with her every night.

"So all this talk about needing to be on his own and figure out what he wants from life was just bullshit. He just didn't want to be married to me."

"April, I don't know," Lilly says. "I feel like Morgan doesn't know what he wants. He's missing something, but doesn't even know what it is. He probably meant it when he said he needed to be on his own. He probably does need to be on his own. But he can't do it, because the thing he's missing is the strength to do what needs to be done."

"Well, he was strong enough to ask for a divorce."

"By text. And then he let you figure out how to sell the house. And I'm guessing you also figured out everything else about divorcing and he just showed up to sign the paperwork. He depended on you."

That's funny. April always thought it was Morgan who gave her strength.

April sits in the post office parking lot for a long while. What can she do to make this awful feeling go away? She'll start with a latte at Tea'd Off. Rebellion is in order, and caffeine is a pretty rebellious thing to consume this late in the day.

Driving past The Diner, April spots Evan's car parked out front. At the stoplight, as she waits on the red, she senses someone watching her. She looks out her driver's side window to see Coach Bashum standing on the corner, staring at her with his steely (literally) eyes.

She gets his message. Fuck caffeine. What April needs is Evan.

She takes an unplanned left and parks on the cross street. After a quick check of her image in the rear-view mirror, she applies some lip gloss, takes a deep breath and exits her car. A little thrill replaces the dread in the pit of her stomach. Now THIS is rebellious.

Morgan has moved on. It's time for April to move on. It's time to have some fun. She's free now. She's free to do anything and anyone she wants. Maybe Morgan needs to jump back into the bonds of a serious relationship, but April is ready to have some awesome sex that isn't bound by anything but attraction.

If that kiss last night is any indication, Evan is good for April. He's present. He's now. And that's where April needs to be. She doesn't want to worry about the past or wonder about the future anymore. Let's get this party started!

As April rounds the corner, she gets a full view of Evan sitting on the front patio of The Diner. He looks gorgeous . . . and so does the woman sitting next to him.

Judging by the woman's body language (unless Evan has an attractive cousin with zero sense of personal space) she is on a date. Which means Evan is on a date. Alice Deeds would not be happy with how close this lady is to Evan. April isn't thrilled about it either.

She stands frozen for a moment, not sure what to do next. She wonders if she can back up slowly and hide behind Coach Basham's sack. As Evan's head begins to turn in her direction, April puts her back to the scene and rushes away.

"April?" his voice calls to her.

Shit. He saw her. Her cheeks fill with the heat of embarrassment. This is adding insult to injury. Her husband is dating someone else and now her booty call is bootying a beautiful woman outside of April's favorite place to eat.

April pretends she doesn't hear Evan shout her name. But another voice calls, "April!"

She turns toward the second voice to see Daniel holding a squeegee in front of the windows of Antic Witties. "I'm almost done." He waves his squeegee in the air as he shouts across the street. "Get us a table. I'll be right there."

April doesn't move as she tries to make heads or tails of her situation. "Or . . ." Daniel continues yelling, "Just come over here!"

"Okay!" April calls across the street. "Okay! I'll just come over there."

She pushes the button for the walk sign at the intersection. Coach B. stands between her and Evan and Evan's date. She side-eyes the statue and whispers, "Asshole." It takes an eternity to get the walk signal. Her heart pounds. She prays Evan won't call out to her again.

She walks stiffly across the street, very aware of her body and trying to imitate how she walks when she's not thinking about how she walks. Once she hits the sidewalk on Daniel's side of the street, she glances at the restaurant. Evan isn't outside anymore.

April approaches Daniel just as he drops the squeegee in a bucket and picks up the entire apparatus by the handle. Water sloshes out as he opens the door to the shop. Not a word passes between them as they enter. Daniel locks the door behind him, then flips the *Open* sign to *Closed*.

As he heads into the bathroom to dump the bucket of water, he says, "One summer in high school, I went to a tennis camp with Evan. I had to hold his feet during sit-ups every morning. He never made it through without farting. Ever."

April laughs before she has a chance to think about it. Her mortification at the events of the last three minutes lessens slightly. She digests this new intel on Evan, and Daniel's motivation in sharing it.

"How did you handle it?" she asks.

"I never told a soul. Didn't even discuss it with him."

"You never acknowledged it? Like with a shared look or something?"

"Never," says Daniel. "I acted like nothing was happening, and I think he was happy to believe I was somehow too stupid to notice."

"Why didn't you ever say anything?"

Daniel shrugs, "Let him have his dignity."

April absorbs this as she takes the lid off a candle and inhales. "Is that what you just did for me? Let me have my dignity?"

"You like that one?" Daniel leans against the door frame of the bathroom as he watches April with the candle.

"Vanilla lavender is still the best, but this is nice," she says as she returns the lid and sets the candle on the table. "Smells like a $47 ocean breeze."

Daniel laughs. It's a very satisfying sound to April.

"Seriously," she says as she reaches for another candle to try. "Were you saving me?"

"You don't need saving. It's one of the things I like about you."

Under the weight of Daniel's compliment, a little more of April's grief and embarrassment dissipate. She's thankful to keep busy with the candles. "Well," she begins slowly, "I'll tell you something else you'll like about me."

"Okay."

April takes on a serious expression. "I don't fart when I do sit-ups."

"Really?!" Daniel replies.

"Nope," she answers. "I don't even do sit-ups. And I hate the word *fart*. It's right up there with *moist*. I have never used either word in my life."

"You don't talk about doing the f word?"

"No. And if I did, I'd call it *gas*."

"So what's the verb form of that? Gassing?"

"Passing gas. My mom called it P.G.'ing for short."

"Please use that in a sentence."

"Who keeps P.G.'ing?" April offers this as an example of a perfectly acceptable sentence about bodily functions.

"P.G.'ing?!" Daniel barely gets the term out. "That would be short for pass gassing."

April has to think about this for a moment. "Oh my god!" Her entire world is shaken. "I never thought of that." She tries to wrap her brain around it. "Passing gas should have been P.'ing G.! My mom taught me wrong!"

April's phone pings with a text message. She stiffens, but makes no motion to reach for the phone in her purse. Instead, she reaches for another candle.

Daniel watches her for a beat. "I'm gonna close the register." He crosses out of the bathroom while wiping the sweat from his neck with a paper towel. He heads toward the counter at the front of the store, intending to give April space to check her phone, but she refuses. She will not jump to her phone to see if Evan has . . . okay, she gives in and reaches for her phone.

Seeing Evan's name on the screen sends a buzz through her that she immediately regrets. Her body has a mind of its own. She tries to maintain a neutral face in case Daniel sees her open the message from Evan.

Evan: Did you hear me calling you? It's prob obvs I'm on a date. Hope that doesn't bother you.

April starts to write back.

April: What are you talking about?

She plans to respond as though she wasn't even aware of Evan or his stupid, impeccably dressed date. Wait. April stops herself from mentally insulting the woman. That woman has done nothing wrong. And honestly, neither has Evan.

April promised herself she'd note any red flags. Evan has lots of them. The

86

thing that makes Evan likable is that he holds his own red flags and waves them in your face. What you see is what you get. Except, apparently, for an acknowledgment of Ping G.

April deletes her response text and pulls herself out of her inner monologue by calling to Daniel, "Can I buy you dinner?"

He closes the cash register and turns to face her. He takes April in for a moment before leaning against the counter. When his hands reach back to support his weight, the muscles peeking out from under his short-sleeve shirt flex. April tries hard to avoid noticing.

"Yes," he says finally, "but not at The Diner please."

"Good," says April. "I hate that place."

15

Another Coach

Dinner at Burger Barn is satisfying and a fraction of the price of The Diner. But April and Daniel both wish adult beverages were served. Their conversation goes in fits and starts. After an hour, it seems there's nothing left to say.

They've already talked about: Daniel's art. Both of them being on crew for *Into the Woods*. Demmy's singing talent.

They've avoided talking about: April's writing. April's divorce. April's ex-husband's new girlfriend.

Now they sit in an extended pause at the picnic table nearest the parking lot.

"Well," April begins the end of the evening, "thank you again for helping me earlier. I appreciated the chance to save my pride."

Daniel looks like he might speak, but he smiles instead.

"What?" April asks.

"I'm aware I sometimes say things out loud I should keep to myself." Daniel loads a plastic tray with their trash from dinner. "I'm trying to be more careful."

This explains the stilted conversation tonight. Daniel is censoring himself. Yes, April has been surprised by his let's-just-lay-it-all-out-there approach in the past, but tonight he's trying to control himself and . . .

"Honestly?" she says. "Careful Daniel is boring."

"Ouch."

"Not ouch. I'm saying the real you is more interesting than the guy who's trying to behave."

"Behave, huh?" Daniel looks at April in a way that catches her off guard. She breaks eye contact and grabs the tray with both hands. Daniel takes it from her. "I got it," he says as he lifts the tray and stands.

April watches Daniel walk to the trashcan to deposit the remains of their dinner. After he slides the tray into the rack next to the can, he picks up two cups abandoned on a table nearby and tosses those, too. Then he stops for a moment to chat with the woman working the walk-up window of Burger Barn and he appears to wave to the cook inside.

When Daniel returns, he walks to April's side of the picnic bench offering his hand. She takes it and struggles to lift both legs up and over the bench. It's hard to straddle seating in a dress. She makes it to her feet.

"Sorry if I flashed too much ankle there," she says.

"Just enough for me to think about all night."

April is joking, of course. Daniel is too, but something about the way he says he'll be thinking of her all night makes April wish Daniel was serious. Their hands fall apart as they walk toward the parking lot.

"Do you . . ." Daniel starts, almost thinks better of it, but proceeds anyway, "miss your ex?"

April gives Daniel a look that says, "How do you go from flirting about ankles to asking about exes?"

Daniel puts his hands up in surrender. "This is me not behaving anymore. You don't have to answer."

April notices little nerves dancing in her stomach. There's a lot of drama to unload on someone she's still getting acquainted with. It's hard to know how much to say.

"It's a strange day to ask me that question."

"Uh oh," Daniel says.

"Yeah, exactly. Uh oh. You may regret asking."

"I won't." He sounds certain as he lowers the tailgate of his truck and sits. April is not so certain. She stays standing. "I found out he's seeing someone."

"Oh shit," says Daniel. "I'm sorry. That's really hard."

His empathy threatens to stir up the emotions April has shoved down into the depths of her bones. She has to look away from the concern on his face. She sits beside him on the truck bed. "It is what it is."

"I miss being married sometimes," says Daniel. "Or, I miss the idea of being married—especially in a crisis. There's no one to share the responsibility. Like when there was an enormous spider in my bathroom the other night, and there was no one to scoop it up and put it outside except me."

"You don't just kill spiders?"

"No. I used to, but one day I looked one of them in his multiple sets of eyes, and I thought—*Shit, he's trying to survive like the rest of us. He has as much a right to live as I do.*"

"How do you know the spider was a he?" asks April.

"All spiders are hes. What? You never had Ms. Hoff for science?"

"Oh, I had Ms. Hoff. And I know for a fact the black widow is a she spider."

Daniel pushes himself further into the bed of his truck and leans his back against the side. His long legs stretch out in front of him. "Ms. Hoff's honors biology was the hardest class I ever took. Much harder than any of my classes in college. What about Tech? They teach any classes harder than Ms. Hoff's?"

April twists to face Daniel. "How do you know I went to Tech?"

"Your bio on the inside cover of your book."

"You bought the actual book?"

"I did. I like the experience of real books."

"Well, thank you." April watches the setting sun. "I'll be expecting my $2 royalty payment in a few months."

There was a time, knowing someone read her book brought April joy. Now it seems cringe worthy, like when, say . . . your mom brings up that talent show you won in sixth grade when you had permed bangs and recited original poetry about love .

"So, does it bother you he's seeing someone else?" Daniel asks.

Geez, this guy flips conversation like an emotional light switch.

"Evan?" April croaks.

"No," Daniel looks rattled, "or maybe him too. But I meant Morgan."

Morgan's name coming out of Daniel's mouth is so strange. Like two worlds colliding. "It's weird for me that you read the book. It's like you've been inside my head, and I hardly know anything about you."

Daniel notices April doesn't answer his question, but he doesn't ask again. "Thousands of people read your book. I'm pretty sure half of Cleo read it."

"Only half?" April pretends to take offense. She doesn't want to explain to Daniel why it makes her uncomfortable that he specifically read the book. She's not sure she knows why the thought of him reading it makes her want to escape her skin.

The sun sets in a brilliant display of colors; pink, orange, purple. It fills the quiet for a time.

Daniel watches April. He likes to think he's pretty good at reading people. So good, in fact, it often gets him into trouble. People don't always enjoy hearing what they are thinking said aloud.

April senses his eyes on her. She turns her face toward his with a heavy sigh. "What?" she asks.

Daniel scoots until his legs dangle off the back of the truck next to April's. "You do know it's a great book?"

April winces before turning her gaze back to the sunset. "The title is terrible," she says.

Daniel pushes his body off the truck and stands facing April. "You. Do. Know. It's a great book. April, it was a bestseller."

"I've read bestsellers that had all the artistry of toilet paper," April responds. She meets Daniel's exasperated expression head on.

"Yeah . . . well, I can think of a thousand times in my life that toilet paper was a hell of a lot more useful than Walt Whitman."

April laughs before she's even aware she's laughing. Being caught in Daniel's focus is like being in the beam of a UFO. You're not sure what the hell is happening, but you're too mesmerized to run away.

Daniel settles back on the edge of the truck, enjoying the sound of April's laughter. "You don't want to talk about the book," Daniel concedes. "But you told me I was boring, so I think I get to tell you one painful truth."

April pulls in a deep breath of Burger Barn scented air. "Alright."

"It is a great story, told by a talented writer. That doesn't change because something happened after that story ended."

"I don't know," says April. "Santa Claus was a great story until it wasn't true anymore."

"But Santa Claus was never true. What you wrote about was real."

Was it, though? Is it? April shrugs. Daniel can't change her mind about this . . . but he's sure going to try.

He stands in frustration. "Do you remember Arnold Talc?"

"The name sounds familiar."

"Talc was this fuck-up, high school kid in CISD class of '84. He never played sports. Never got involved with any school organizations. Never even came to a football game. He was just existing through high school. Well, he goes to junior college because his parents threaten to kick him out of the house if he doesn't, and he gets a job as the manager of the football team. Then he transfers and manages the team at Tarleton State."

April interrupts, "Is this Rudy? Are you just telling me the Texas version of Rudy?"

"No," Daniel insists. "This is a true story. Just listen."

"I am listening. That's how I know it sounds like Rudy."

Daniel ignores April's efforts to distract him. "So this guy Talc manages the football team at his college and suddenly, it turns out, he loves the game and he's good at it. Really good. Not playing, but coaching. (See? Not like Rudy.) So he graduates with his degree in sports science and he comes back to CISD in '89 as the assistant football coach. Two weeks into the season, the head football coach has a stroke and retires."

"Oh no."

"Don't worry, he's fine. He goes on to own a lawn business and makes bank. So Talc becomes head coach and his boys on the team, they love him. They adore him because he doesn't relate to them like this high-ranking coach mentoring players. He reaches them as one screw up to another. So guess what?"

"They win."

"Not only do they win, they win the State Championship of 1989. The first time in the school's history. Only five years after this bastard leaves the high school without ever even giving a shit about football, with no one knowing who he was, he comes back and leads the freaking team to victory."

"That's cool."

"It is cool! It's a great story, right?"

"It's a good story," April says.

"It's a great story," Daniel counters.

"But . . . " April rolls her wrist to encourage Daniel to get on with it.

"No buts. Great story." Daniel pauses for a long moment. "No matter what happened next, that championship trophy is real. It still sits in the trophy case at the high school. Great story."

"Daniel," April says, "just tell me what happened next."

"Not that it matters, because the original story is still a great story." Daniel smiles. "But two years later, Talc gets fired for getting drunk and pissing on the principal's porch."

"No."

"Yes. He gets fired. He takes a quiet position at the bank where his mom works and he never reaches for glory again in his whole life."

"What happened?! If my dad ever won a state championship, I'm pretty sure he would have that fact carved into his gravestone. He coached for twenty years and never won a big one."

"How many writers do you think have written for twenty years and never had a bestseller?" Daniel asks.

Well, she walked right into that one. April answers with a tired look.

"I'm just saying I think about Talc a lot," Daniel says. "How he caught lightning in a bottle. And, instead of being proud of that, he was ashamed he couldn't make it happen again. So he pissed away all these other opportunities—literally." Daniel's hand drops to his side, and when it does, the length of his arm touches April's. Goosebumps travel from her wrist to her shoulder. "But that '89 Championship, that's a great story."

The Texas sky does not disappoint as the sun slips lower on the horizon. The crickets are singing the first set of their nightly concert.

April tries to decide whether it's a smart idea to say what she's saying as she says it. "I know it's contrite. I know there are so many bigger problems in the world, and I must seem ungrateful. But I'm not. I'm . . ."

As she searches for the right word, the one word she's trying to avoid is the one that escapes her lips.

"Embarrassed."

There it is. The truth.

Daniel's expression looks pained. "Well, that's a damn shame."

16

For the Kids

The annual fundraiser for the Cleo Education Foundation is a formal event held at the community center. It features a nice dinner followed by local entertainment vying for the most votes. Tickets to the event are $100. Each vote is $5.

April bought a new dress just for the occasion. It's got a vintage vibe per her usual style, but it's form fitting—hugging her curves in a way she's not used to. Demmy talked her into it.

April feels good in the dress—the glass of wine she had while getting ready helps too. Honoring both the large hair of her Texas roots and the 1940s style, she sweeps her hair up in big pin curls. The dress is a deep purple, a color that a psychic once told April was her power color.

When she gives a last look in the mirror before leaving her house, she likes the woman she sees there, even if she doesn't quite know who she is yet.

April has been in Cleo long enough to unpack her boxes. She even moved the dresser in her bedroom to the correct spot on the wall. (Of course, the dresser is still in the box waiting to be put together, but now the box sits in the right spot.) April's online class is going well, and downtown Cleo is getting decorated for the holidays.

Just before the shopping rush of the season, the Education Foundation hosts their big fundraiser. April and Demmy are here to enjoy the evening.

Evan spots Demmy and April as soon as they enter the event center. April hasn't seen him in the few weeks since the on-a-date-with-another-woman incident. But late that night, after April arrived home from having Burger Barn with Daniel, Evan sent a text.

Evan: Don't be mad at me, Townsend. Hope you have sweet dreams.

And, though she wished it didn't change things, April found that the text erased most of the sting she felt toward Evan. She's happy to see him looking gorgeous as ever as he approaches.

"You both look stunning," he says as he greets Demmy and April with a quick kiss on the cheek, but he is not the usual effusive flirt. "The Carvers are sick," he tells Demmy. "Both of them got a stomach bug."

Demmy looks worried. "You're kidding."

"Who are the Carvers?" April asks.

"Well, Carl Carver was supposed to co-host with me and Elaine Carver was one of our contestants," answers Evan.

"Oh no," says April, "can you host by yourself?"

"I'm hoping I don't have to." He looks pointedly at April. When his intention is clear, Demmy looks pointedly at April, too.

"Not me." April shakes her head.

"You've spoken to crowds of hundreds of people," Demmy says.

"Not in years," says April.

Evan grabs her hand. "April, please. The script is written for two people."

Well, so much for a fun night. Now it's going to be a nerve-racking night of work.

"There's a script?" April asks.

Evan knows he's got her. "All the introductions are written on note cards."

"I haven't rehearsed."

Demmy does her part to persuade her friend. "The audience will know you're filling in. They'll be so forgiving. And it's for the kids."

"The kids," Evan emphasizes.

April looks back and forth between Demmy and Evan, both of them giving their most earnest looks. "Okay," April gives in. "But you still need another singer?"

"Yes, do you sing too?" Evan asks.

"I don't," April emphasizes the "I" as she looks pointedly at Demmy. Touché.

"April!" Demmy says her friend's name like she's saying, "Don't be ridiculous."

"Demmy!" April returns the tone.

Demmy tries another tactic. "I don't have music. I'm not sure I know all the lyrics to any song."

Evan cuts in, "Cathy Patterson is our accompanist. She can download sheet music to her tablet and the woman can sight read anything. And you can hold your phone with the lyrics or I'll write them out myself on note cards."

"The audience will be so forgiving. It's for the kids." April smiles.

"Shit," is Demmy's version of yes.

Demmy gets whisked off to meet with Cathy Patterson. Evan directs April across the stage and through the curtain into the small backstage. They huddle close together, trying to read Evan's single set of note cards. Both of them are too focused on the task at hand to think about how close their bodies are to one another. Well, mostly too focused to notice that they are so close, they're actually touching in several places.

A voice behind them makes them jump as though they're caught doing something they shouldn't. Evan and April turn to find Daniel peering through the curtain. "Oh, sorry," he mumbles as he turns to leave.

"No, wait." April follows him onto the stage. She doesn't want Daniel to misread the situation, especially after he saved her from Evan once before. "I'm co-hosting. I'm filling in for Carl."

"He's sick. Elaine too," Evan chimes in from the other side of the curtain.

"We were just reading the intros off note cards. Evan only has one set."

You know how sometimes people are as bad at telling the truth as they are at lying? Somehow, April's truth sounds a lot like a cover up of something more nefarious.

Daniel nods, but April can't tell if he believes her story. "I'll get you a script," he says as he walks across the stage.

For fear she'll sound even more suspicious, April stops from elaborating on the truth. Instead, she calls after Daniel, "Thank you!"

An hour later, the crowd finishes dinner. April is too nervous to eat the $100 meal she paid for, but she eats a roll Daniel brings her after Evan brings her a second glass of wine (technically third, if one is counting the glass April had while dressing). Daniel also brings water, which suggests he's concerned about April being tipsy onstage.

But his worries are unnecessary. April has been in many dozens of backstages filled with champagne and treats. She's learned the art of accepting food and drink and discreetly depositing them anywhere but her stomach.

She hands off Evan's first glass of wine to Demmy (who needs a little relaxer). Then she waters a plant backstage with the second glass of wine. Unfortunately, she discovers too late that the plant is fake. So she waters a plastic plant. Well, technically she wines a plastic plant.

Now she paces backstage, going over the script.

Daniel scanned the note cards onto April's phone and set them up in a file that's easy to access. He, as it turns out, is the stage manager for the performance portion of the evening. Thus, he is stuck problem solving script issues and monitoring the alcohol level of the performers. Apparently, this is the task he takes on every year for this fundraiser. He's quite good at the logistics of corralling less than sober singers.

He does it for the kids.

Evan takes the stage solo to begin the introductions and explain the change in lineup. Daniel stands stage left by the dressing rooms, watching April in the wings opposite of him. She's staring at her phone, studying her first lines, when a text from Daniel pops up.

Daniel: You'll be great.

April looks up to see Daniel watching her from across the stage. He waves. She waves.

They've seen each other twice since Burger Barn. Once at Tea'd Off, where April was working on her writing course curriculum, and once when April ran into the antique store to ask for directions to a notary public she couldn't find. (It turned out the woman relocated months ago and never bothered to change her address online because everyone in town knew where she'd

98

moved to.)

Daniel looks down at his phone to message her again.

Daniel: When you exit the stage, come to me. I'll get you set up for the next intro.

April: Don't let me fuck this up, Daniel.

Daniel: I'll do my best.

Evan introduces April to the crowd, and Daniel is privileged to be the only person in the world who gets to witness this transformation from regular April to this other April. Like watching Clark Kent take off his glasses, Daniel watches April erase the stress from her face as she tucks her phone between her breasts.

Whatever small insecurities April may have in that form fitting dress, she releases them into the dark corners of backstage right. She pulls a confidence up from the stage floor, through her high heels and into the curves of her thighs. Then up to the cleavage housing her cell phone. Up through her long, elegant throat. And finally, up to a wide, genuine grin as she steps out from behind the curtain to greet the audience.

Before the crowd gets to see that smile, April gives it to Daniel first. He feels the impact of it just like being punched in the chest.

17

There is a House in Cleo

Now, Evan makes a good host because he enjoys being the center of attention. He is charming—at least as much as anyone can be charming when they are trying to be.

April, it seems to Daniel, is impressive on a different level. She's magnetic. There's a confidence in the way she presents herself that puts the audience at ease. She makes a quip as soon as she enters the stage light and Daniel sees the crowd relax back into their seats with smiles on their faces.

She sells the vote fundraising to the audience in the most palatable way. Where Evan teases people into donating, April is passionate in her description of where their money will go and what it means. She speaks so expertly about the Education Foundation, no one listening would know she only just learned all these things from reading the script prior to walking out on the stage.

Daniel wishes he attended one of April's talks when she toured with the book. He enjoys watching the audience watch her, how they hang on her every word. How they smile when she smiles. Laugh when she jokes. Give money when she asks.

Now, he understands better the power she wields over her audience, and why she's cautious about her own influence. He wonders if April's hesitance to praise her accomplishments comes from a lack of understanding her power, or from a place of really understanding her power and feeling a deep obligation to her audience to lead them in the right direction.

April is captivating onstage, but it's the moments of vulnerability she shows only to Daniel that he enjoys the most.

It's only to Daniel that she drops the stage presence between introductions. She makes funny faces as she exits the stage. To calm her nerves, she rocks on her feet while waiting in the wings. When he hands her a bottle of water, he sees her hand shake slightly as she tips it to her mouth.

This does something to him. It takes effort to stop himself from grabbing her hand to hold it steady.

Daniel is flattered when April asks for his reassurance several times.

He answers the same each time she asks. "You're doing great."

By the fourth time he uses the word *great*, he wants to smack himself in the head. There are other descriptive words, but the truth is, he's afraid to tell her what he really thinks. What's he going to say? "It's an honor to witness you onstage"? Or "I'm happy to watch you wipe your sweaty hands on your thighs"? No. He's sticking to *great*.

They get into a routine. Evan and April meet onstage. They banter back and forth; some of it is scripted, some not. Then they exit opposite sides. April comes to Daniel to regroup and greet the next contestant on stage left. Evan retreats to the solitary space of stage right—where he can focus on himself.

Demmy arrives backstage several performances ahead of her own. She's been rehearsing her song in the echoes of the bathroom through most of the show. She hides behind the curtain legs upstage, observing the other performers from a distance. Demmy is not at all surprised by April's abilities as a host.

What is surprising is her friend Daniel's performance abilities. He is enthralled as he watches April onstage. But, as soon as April stops her performance, Daniel begins his. His smile disappears the moment April turns to exit his direction. He transforms into a stage manager, instead of a man fascinated by the woman standing in front of him.

It worries Demmy to see Daniel so impressed by April. It also warms her heart to see him this way. It's been a long time since Daniel had anyone to be impressed by.

And, of course, April is very impressive. She's also very hurt. And Demmy knows a thing or two about the mistakes people make when they are hurting.

When Demmy moves to the wings just before her number, April drapes an arm over her shoulders as they both stare out at the stage.

"I can't wait to see what you do out there." April whispers.

"You and me both," says Demmy.

Tara Farmer is currently on stage hula-hooping. She's mesmerizing, and April can't help but peek at the other side of the stage to see if Tara mesmerizes Evan. Apparently she doesn't. He's staring at his phone. But Daniel watches Tara. April wonders if he's equally attracted to women who control hula-hoops as to those who control batons.

As Demmy takes the stage, April introduces her friend to enthusiastic applause from the crowd. From the moment Demmy begins her performance, she has the audience with her.

While Demmy sings "House of the Rising Sun", April transports back twenty-five years to the first time she stood backstage watching Demmy perform. April was just an aimless girl then; didn't know who she was or what she should do.

Just like now.

There's one section of the song that hits April hard.

Well, I got one foot on the platform
The other foot on the train
I'm goin' back to New Orleans
To wear that ball and chain

18

The Dance

I have always been a big-boned gal. I had what my mother describes as "delicious rolls" of chub on my arms and knees as a baby.

I believe I was only eight when I fell asleep in the back of my father's car on a late ride home from one of my sister's softball games, and instead of carrying me into the house where I could magically wake up in my bed, Dad had to shake me awake and make me walk myself inside because I'd outgrown his arm strength.

By the time I was ten, I was the permanent base to my older sister's top while playing chicken fight in the pool. Puberty, of course, solidified my tallness and my hippy hips and my broad shoulders. It did not, unfortunately, bring me the breasts to match.

By the time I was twelve, my size ten feet had the choice of a couple pairs of ugly shoes hidden in the back of the stockroom. Truly! When I was growing up, shoe manufacturers had never heard of a girl with a shoe size larger than eight. I bought men's shoes all the time.

Like a lot of teen girls, I wished my body was different, mostly because I wanted to swing dance. On one of the news shows my eighth-grade year, my mom taped a segment on swing dancing. Watching it, I felt a thump in my chest I hadn't felt for anything since reading A Wrinkle in Time *by Madeleine L'Engle in the fourth grade.*

I felt the music and bounce of the dancers. I found it fascinating how they connected. The way the men could lift the women and fly them around like they weighed nothing—like they were easy to carry, I wanted to feel that for myself.

But I knew I never would. I was, at thirteen, taller than every boy in my class. I weighed more too—I was certain. My own dad couldn't pick me up when I was eight.

No boy could lug me around. I'd never be a character in a Jane Austen novel either, because no Mr. Darcy could carry my bottom-of-the-pyramid body type home after I passed out on a long walk in the rain. And I'd never know what it's like to fly in the arms of a man I'm dancing with.

I was too heavy to be swept off my feet.

Excerpt from *Great Expectations* by April Townsend

Demmy doesn't get the most votes, but she consumes the most post-show praise amongst the fundraiser crowd.

Evan works the room. The rest of those involved with the entertainment portion of the event huddle around several tables, drinking the remaining alcohol and eating the leftover desserts they were too nervous to eat before the show. They are relieved, relaxed and tipsy as they bask in the after-show-glow and the $125,000 they raised for the kids.

The crowd is thinning, but the band plays on and those remaining are dancing. April is more talkative than usual as she's on that performance high. She'd forgotten about this buzz. It's nice.

She's entertaining her table with several tales of crazy fans at book signings and a disturbing story about a party for which she was the hired "entertainment" at a dinner in Bel Aire with only two guests.

Daniel enjoys the glimpses into April's other life—the one she rarely discusses and would seemingly prefer to forget. It's fun to watch her talk about it now without the usual preface of her perceived failures.

Demmy seems to read his thoughts. She leans in to Daniel as April tells an animated story across the table that has those around her in stitches, especially Evan—who has just joined the group. Evan puts his arm around April's shoulders and pulls her into his chest as he laughs.

"Do you know what I remember about April in high school?" says Demmy.

Daniel is happy for an excuse to turn away from watching Evan and April.

He looks to Demmy with his eyebrows raised in anticipation.

"She was on crew for *Into the Woods*," Demmy continues.

"She told me that. I don't remember her working on that show at all," Daniel confesses. "It seems like it would be impossible to not notice her."

"Well," says Demmy, "she wasn't her yet. But I got a glimpse of who she'd be. She hardly said two words throughout rehearsals. And then one day I sing through "Giants in the Sky" and everyone loves it and Mrs. Goodman has no notes for me. But I walk past this freshman girl and she says, 'Have you ever admired something that could hurt you?' And then I understood the song. I'd been so focused on hitting the notes, I'd never stopped to consider what the song is really about."

"What is it about?" Daniel takes a drink of his beer as he waits for the point of Demmy's story. He suspects he won't like it.

"Well, I thought it was a song about fear, but it's actually a song about something much scarier than fear."

"Love?" asks Daniel.

"Lack of fear," Demmy answers.

Daniel pauses for the length of one breath before he responds, "I'll never forget the way you sang that song. Damn, you were good. You still are." Demmy looks toward Evan and April. Daniel follows her gaze. "Which one should I be afraid of?" he asks.

"The one that makes you want to break out in a song."

Daniel laughs, "I don't plan on turning my life into a musical anytime soon."

Evan stands and extends his hand toward April. "Come dance with me." April opens her mouth to protest, but he insists, "We're celebrating. Come on."

April can't help herself. She glances at Daniel as she pushes her chair back from the table to stand. She's embarrassed to have him witness her giving into Evan. Daniel already helped snatch April's dignity from Evan's clutches once. She doesn't want to appear to be one of those women who constantly sets herself up to be let down. And, of course, deep down, she hopes she isn't one of those women.

But Daniel meets her glance with a shit-eating grin spread across his face. It easily spreads to April because she knows exactly what he's thinking. Now she can't look Evan in the eyes as he puts his arm around her waist and lifts her other hand in his. She has to look over his shoulder and bite her lip as they sway to the slow music. All she can picture is a young Evan attempting sit-ups.

His words are sobering. "I think we make a good team."

April formulates a safe response before she speaks. "Tonight worked well."

"You were brilliant."

"You did well, too."

"And you look incredible tonight," he says as he pulls her in closer, their bodies in full contact now.

Evan smells fantastic, like cologne. April doesn't know which kind, but she can tell he's been strategic with the quantity—applying just enough so she can only smell it on his neck when he's this close to her. And being this close to him is intoxicating. His good looks, and his good smells, and his good charms are harder to fight with her brain swimming in merlot, but April is still aware Daniel is here.

April did shave tonight, so she can't trust herself fully with Evan. This was all an unexpected turn of events. She was not supposed to host tonight, especially not with Evan. She was not supposed to be dancing with him, especially after several glasses of wine, with her shaved body parts in dangerous proximity to him. But as long as Daniel is here, April will maintain her dignity and a level head. She won't embarrass herself in front of Daniel. He'll be her chastity belt tonight.

She looks over at Daniel's table to see if he's watching. He's not. He's not even there. She spots him walking toward the front with Demmy. He's putting his jacket on.

Oh shit. Her chastity is walking out the door.

April's heart sinks. She's disappointed he's leaving, both because she hates that dancing with Evan is the last thing he sees her doing and because now she's dancing with Evan with no barrier between them.

Evan's in his usual form now. He whispers in April's ear, "You feel so good."

106

April laughs. Evan pulls back to check her face. "What?" he asks. "Too much?"

"Much too much," she replies. He smiles and maneuvers her into a spin under his arm. When he pulls her back to him, he whispers, "You feel so awful. I hate this."

Evan is too charming, but the fact he can make fun of himself for trying too hard to be charming makes him somehow even more charming. His lines don't work on April but his sense of humor does. She's about to lose her will to resist and just relax into him when a voice cuts into their dance. "Evan, the valet people need to see you out front." April turns to see Daniel, his jacket still on.

"It's not my Beamer, is it?" Evan lets go of April in a panic for his car. It's almost comical how her arms flop to her sides as he discards them.

"I don't know," Daniel says. "The guy just asked if I knew whose car it was and I said I'd get you."

Evan takes off without a word to April. She and Daniel lock eyes and smile at his sudden departure. "Well, I guess we're done dancing," she shrugs.

"He's done dancing," says Daniel. He offers April his left hand. "Would you dance with me?"

He's saving her dignity . . . again. Saving her from another man's balls . . . again. Saving her from herself . . . again. She's disappointed he has to. Her chest tightens in embarrassment as she puts her right hand into his left.

"Yes."

Daniel pulls April in close with his right hand on the small of her back. "You remember how to two step?"

"It's been so long."

"It's like riding a bike," assures Daniel as he puts pressure on her back and leads her into a four-step maneuver that has them turn a full circle around each other before falling into the two-steps-forward, one-step-back rhythm of the Texas Two-Step.

The last time April did this dance was with her father at Lilly's wedding. That was over a decade ago.

April discovers pretty quickly that for her, two stepping isn't like riding a bike. It's like trying to balance on the handlebars of a bike she is not pedaling. It's about putting her body in someone else's hands and trusting he will lead her in the right direction. It's about giving over control. None of which April is comfortable doing at this point in her life.

When Evan danced, he just rocked back and forth. April can rock back and forth. This is different. April can't predict Daniel's movement and her legs keep getting tangled with his. The third time it happens, they pause to regroup. Daniel pulls April to a safe spot away from the other couples moving in a wide circle around the dance floor.

"You are going to have to trust me," he says.

"I do trust you. I don't trust myself," April responds.

"Well, you're going to have to start doing that, too." Daniel removes his jacket and tosses it over a chair. "We can do this. I have faith in us."

April takes her heels off and tosses them aside. "Okay," she says. "Let's do it."

Daniel moves closer to her. "Okay. You ready?"

"I'm ready," she says. And she sounds so confident, she almost believes herself.

This time, when Daniel pulls April in, he leaves no space between their bodies. They are ear to ear, chest to chest, belt buckle to belly.

April's feet alternate with Daniel's feet. His right leg nestles between her knees. And for a few beats, he doesn't move. He just holds her like that as she watches couples whirling around them over his shoulder. Her heartbeat speeds up. Her shoulders tense.

She's going to screw this up.

When Daniel takes in a breath, his chest rises against hers. April flinches, trying to anticipate his first step. "Dammit!"

Daniel's fingers spread wider on the small of her back. "April, I'm in charge right now." Daniel laughs softly in her ear.

April drops her shoulders in a way that would make Lilly proud. "Okay," she says as she wiggles her body to get it to loosen up.

"Say it," he whispers.

The thrill of his low voice in her ear has April's heart pounding so hard, there's no way Daniel doesn't feel it thumping against his chest.

"You're in charge, Daniel."

April stills her body and takes a deep breath. As she lets it out, Daniel begins to move her around the floor again. She closes her eyes and tries with all her might to let her mind go blank, to give her body over to Daniel.

She imagines that feeling she had as a kid. That feeling of her father lifting her out of the car to take her to bed. That feeling of her mom spinning her in circles until her feet lifted off the ground. That feeling of being light enough for someone else to carry her.

Then she has it. Daniel pulls her body into a spin against his. They're turning circles around each other fast enough that she doesn't have time to think. Daniel is a gravitational force, taking her wherever he goes.

And for just the briefest moment, both her feet leave the ground at the same time. For that second, she's one of those Jane Austen characters who can be carried a long distance in the rain. She's one of those girls in swing dance getting flown around the room.

Daniel moves April around the dance floor as though she's easy to carry. As though she's no burden at all.

19

Under Wraps

Okay. So nothing about the evening of the fundraiser went according to plan. Not the hosting part. The Evan part. The Daniel, who was supposed to be the savior of April's chastity for the night, literally sweeping her off her feet part.

And definitely not the part where Daniel walked April to her car. Said he wanted to ask her something. Got her stomach all fluttery. Then asked her if she would ever consider . . . coming to work for him at the store during the holidays for $15 an hour.

It was so out of the blue, April didn't know how to react. She asked for more time to consider it.

Now it's Sunday morning and April has driven all the way to the coffee shop off the highway to avoid the risk of running in to anyone in town. She needs to talk to someone about this offer from Daniel. Someone else has to hear this shit. She can't call Demmy because Demmy has too many opinions about April and Daniel already.

So, April's on the phone with Lilly. She's at the part of the story where Daniel has walked her to her car.

"Then, he asks me to work in his store wrapping purchases!" April talks hands free in her car as she drives back home with a steaming cup of coffee in her cup holder. There's a long pause on her sister's end of the line.

"Like gift wrapping?" Lilly sounds incredulous.

"Yes, gift wrapping!"

Lilly laughs and April is thankful someone else finds it absurd. She's a college graduate and a published author. And Daniel asked her to do something a teenager could easily do.

"What in the world makes him think you'd be good at that?" Lilly continues laughing.

Yeah, exactly . . . wait . . . "What?" April sputters.

"Christmas morning everyone knows the gifts from you because they look like a toddler wrapped them."

Ouch.

April is silent as Lilly keeps laughing. And keeps laughing. Eventually, the big sister notices the silence on the other end of the line. "April? Did I lose you?"

"Yes." April's reply is deadpan.

"I don't get it." Lilly stops laughing. "I thought we found it amusing that Daniel assumes you can wrap presents."

April's response is clipped. "Forget it."

"No, don't do that. That's not fair. I'm sorry if I misunderstood."

"I have a college degree. I'm a published author." Even as April says the things in her head out loud, she squirms at the sound of her ego.

"Oh, I see," says Lilly. "You're offended the guy who runs an antique store didn't offer you a book deal."

"It's embarrassing." There's that word again. Embarrass. That's been coming up a lot lately. "It's a job you offer a high schooler , not a . . ." She can't finish the sentence.

"Not a what?"

April has not felt proud being the divorced author of an autobiographical romance novel, but apparently she's proud enough to be insulted by another job offer. She changes course. "Not a woman you just danced with like you were trying to melt her clothes off."

"So the dancing was more than friendly?"

"I mean, I'm rusty at this. I don't know." April rests her head against the headrest of her driver's seat as she pulls into her own driveway. "It's possible

I just can't read him. Maybe he'd dance that way with his employee. Maybe he'd dance that way with his mom."

"So he wants to melt his mother's clothes off?"

The corners of April's mouth try to swing upward, but she forces them back down. She is annoyed, and she will not allow herself to smile while annoyed.

"Alright," says April. "Enough questions. I don't need a therapist. I need a sister."

"Okay. Here's my sisterly advice," says Lilly. "You don't have to accept the work, but you shouldn't be offended by the offer. Daniel works at that antique store. Maybe he doesn't see it as a second-rate job."

"He co-owns the store! I'd be the part-time help. And I'm not even trusted with the register or sales. I don't even deal with the customers. I just get shoved in the back by myself to wrap things up with a pretty bow."

"I'm not hearing the downside to this job," says Lilly.

April sounds defensive, which is often a sign of not wanting her sister to be right. "What makes him think I even need a job?"

"You do need a job," Lilly says as a matter of fact.

"I have work. Thank you very much. I'm teaching an online class." The class doesn't pay enough to live on, but April's not willing to admit that at the moment.

Lilly attempts a more gentle approach. "Look at it like this. Worst-case scenario, Daniel wonders if you'd like a job wrapping presents because you're a creative person. Sounds like a fun and pretty simple job paying better than a lot of harder jobs. And at the end of the day, you get to leave and not check emails or take phone calls all hours of the night, which sounds pretty appealing to me right now as I'm already fielding calls and emails about a meeting tomorrow morning. Best-case scenario, he's a cute guy who wants to spend some time with you. And he doesn't know how to ask you out, so he asked you to work for him instead."

But that's one thing bothering April about the offer. Hiring someone screams, "You're co-worker material." And co-worker material is even a step below friend material. And April kind of liked believing she'd moved up into dirty dancing material last night.

Maybe she's not offended by Daniel's job offer. Maybe she's hurt by his rejection.

20

Storm's a Brewin'

It's pouring rain. April ducks into Antic Witties on her way home from a coffee meeting with the Gales to discuss the arts non-profit. They mentioned twice they can't believe April and Daniel hadn't met prior to the gallery pop-up.

Daniel is busy with a customer when April sets off the front door bell on her entrance to the shop. He waves to her, "I'll be right with you."

April wanders into the wedding registry area of the back room. Her wet shoes squeak as she walks. She recognizes one bride-to-be as Mimi, the college grad Evan introduced her to at the pop-up. She's marrying a guy she met her very first day of college. Their registry items are on display in a large antique cupboard in the small back room.

April looks at their everyday-use dishes, their candlesticks, their table runner; all very reasonably priced. Across the room is another couple's display; serving dishes, a crystal punch bowl, place settings at $100 a piece—shit people never end up using. Plus, they have a $150 throw blanket.

A $150 blanket?! April thinks. *That better be the best fucking blanket this side of the Guadalupe.* Of course, she doesn't actually remember where the Guadalupe is located.

April hears the bell on the front door and soon Daniel appears in the doorway of the registry room.

"Did you make a sale?" she asks.

114

"No. Actually, the weather looks bad. She wanted to make it home before it gets worse." Daniel moves to a window on the back wall and opens the shade. It's gray outside with an ominous low hanging block of a cloud in the western sky.

"I should do the same." April crosses to peer out the window but keeps several steps back from Daniel.

"I think you missed your chance. It floods quickly around here."

The water is already halfway up the tires on a car parked in the alley. April frowns, "Shoot." She did not intend to spend time with Daniel. She just wanted to run in and turn down the job.

"It usually passes quickly," Daniel tries to assure her, but the alarm sounding on his phone doesn't sound reassuring. "Tornado watch," he says as he reads the alert.

"I don't even remember," April says as she moves closer to Daniel to get a better view of the low hanging cloud. "A watch is just looking for it right? And a warning means take cover?"

"Right," Daniel says. "We'll take cover under the stairs if the sirens go off."

"Sounds cozy." April's attempt at humor comes across stiff and creepy. She's not sure if she's more nervous about a tornado warning or being alone under the stairs with Daniel. The pair turn away from the window to face the room of wedding registries. "I'd forgotten how quickly the weather turns here," April says.

Daniel hears the nerves in her voice and tries to distract her. "Since reading your book, I can't come into this room without fear of finding someone humping a bowl."

"That's what you took from that chapter? Just that visual?" April asks.

"You have to admit, it was quite a visual."

Thunder claps. Daniel checks his phone for updates on the weather. April keeps busy by inspecting the linen napkins on the fancy couple's registry. April and Morgan registered for cloth napkins and used them exactly once, and even then, it was just out of guilt for having made friends purchase such an ostentatious item.

"Do you know," starts April, "out of all the chapters of my book, that strip show is the one thing that's brought up to me the most?"

"Really?"

"Yes. Men comment on it because it's funny and women comment on it because it's not."

Daniel is thoughtful for a moment. "Do you think it's funny?"

"I didn't know what to make of it at the time I wrote about it."

"And now?"

"And now I enjoy the singular sensation of doing my own dishes," April smiles pointedly at Daniel, "and only when I'm in the mood to do so."

Daniel returns her smile just as the sirens wale outside. "That's it," he says as he and April both jump to attention. Daniel grabs the blanket from the fancy registry table and April follows him toward the middle of the store.

Daniel moves an upended bed frame to reveal a door under the stairs. Most of the ceilings in the store are two stories high, but there's a small storage loft over the area with the candles and the bear table. Daniel's phone alert buzzes again. The noise on the high ceiling of the English antiques room increases.

Daniel pauses and looks up. "Hail!" he observes. But with his Texas accent, it sounds like Daniel says, "Hell!"

This startles April. "What?! What is it?!"

"What is what?"

"You said 'hell'," April points out.

With Daniel's Texas ear, he believes April just said "hail". So he replies, "Yes."

This frustrates April. "Why? Why did you say hell?"

"Because it IS hail."

"WHAT is hell?"

"Hail is chunks of ice that fall from the sky!" Daniel says this as though April has lost her mind. Can living in Southern California for twenty years make one forget other weather phenomena?

April's hands spring to cover her mouth. Her eyes give away her amusement, even if her hands could muffle her laughter—which they can't.

"I'm sorry. I'm sorry," she declares between giggles. "You're talking about hail. H.A.I.L. But with your accent, I thought you were saying 'hell'. Like, 'Oh hell! The roof is going to fall in!'"

Daniel is not amused. "Okay. Can we get in the closet now?"

Oh hell. She's embarrassed him. April hasn't seen this version of Daniel before. He attempts to be cold, but he hands April the warm blanket from his arms. April's nervous giggles burst forth again. Daniel walks away. "Go in. I'll grab a candle," he calls over his shoulder.

"What am I supposed to do with the blanket?"

Daniel turns to see if she is serious. "Sit on it."

"It's $150," she argues. "The floor is all dirty in there!" She points to the cement at the bottom of the closet under the stairs.

"Thus, the blanket," says Daniel as he leaves her to figure it out for herself. "I've got to get the candle."

April wants to suggest they just use the flashlight on their phones instead of a candle, but it doesn't seem like the right time to present an alternate idea.

The headroom at the entrance of the closet is fine for standing, but it diminishes quickly. April has to go to her hands and knees to fit in the small space along the back wall without hitting her head on the underside of the stairs. She lays out the throw blanket as she apologizes to it for slumming it on the dirty floor.

She crawls to the far corner. April's uncontrolled laughter from a moment ago turns into an uneasy silence. Daniel is taking his time returning, and April regrets laughing at his accent.

"I'm sorry," she calls toward the door of the closet. "I'm just nervous." When Daniel doesn't respond, April decides on a peace offering. She embarrassed him and now she'll embarrass herself. "You're lucky, actually. When I'm nervous, I'm either laughing or P.'ing G."

At that exact moment, Daniel appears in the doorway with a towel, a candle and an expression April can't discern. He ducks into the crawl space, revealing another figure behind him.

Alice. Alice Deeds stands framed in the doorway under the stairs. She's wearing a gorgeous blouse and a tight skirt with heels. She's soaking wet, making her blouse a bit see through. It's a lot hotter look than April's hoodie.

"What's P.'ing G.?" Alice asks as she enters the closet behind Daniel and closes the door.

"Oh, uh, just something dumb," April answers. Luckily, Alice gets distracted by the towel Daniel passes to her.

Daniel attempts to make eye contact with April as he explains Alice's presence, but he can't do so without laughing. So he has to look slightly past April even as addresses her.

"Alice is here. She came in from the storm."

"I can see that," April says.

Daniel presses his lips together and stares straight ahead, concentrating mightily on keeping himself from indulging in the sweet karma of April's bad timing.

"I'm April," April says while reaching her arm across Daniel in order to extend her hand to Alice.

Alice looks turned off by the offer as she holds her red hair in the towel to keep it from dripping. Her lips tremble a bit from the cold. She slips a freezing hand into April's grasp.

"I know who you are. Everyone does." Alice doesn't mean anything offensive by that comment. At least, April doesn't think she does.

Alice concentrates on her phone wholeheartedly. Which would be fine with April, if it wasn't so damn quiet under the stairs. Her entire life, she has never overcome the need to end silence.

Daniel lights the candle with a lighter. He chose the vanilla scent. April can't help but think of a magazine article she read once about an olfactory experiment that endeavored to discover what scents turn men and women on. Women got hot and bothered by the smell of baby powder. Men preferred vanilla.

April dismissed the study. The "scientists" had to be a bunch of men who expected women to like the smell of babies and thus prejudiced their results. But that didn't explain why they assumed men would find vanilla erotic.

Vanilla. The least exotic of the flavorings. Was that really what men craved? Luke-warm, mild, safe vanilla?

There's no telling how long this thought process overtakes April's mind, but when she finally looks up from the candle flame, she notices Alice Deeds is wearing Daniel's sweater. *InDEED she is.* April is proud of herself for keeping that pun inside her head. She is not proud of how she feels seeing Daniel's sweater on Alice.

She squirms in discomfort. It's just too fucking noiseless in the closet, and Alice is just too fucking in Daniel's clothes . . . "Both our names start with an *"A"* and have five letters!"

Well, that's that. April has ended the silence and replaced it with something worse.

In synchronized slow motion, Alice and Daniel's puzzled expressions turn to shine on April. She withers in their stares, "I just . . . it just occurred to me, Alice, that both our names start with an *"A".* Actually, they both have an *"L"* too! And an *"I"* for that matter! We share a lot of common letters of the alphabet in our names."

So what? April panic thinks. *So now we're soul sisters or something, because we share letters?!*

Alice's phone buzzes with a text. Thank god. Alice stops listening to April's ramblings and checks her message. Daniel, however, is not so kind. He stares at April. His eyes say, "What in the world are you talking about?" But his tight smile says, "I'm really enjoying watching you babble uncomfortably."

Damn him. He's no help at all.

"She's here," Alice says as she attempts to stand up in her tight skirt.

"I've got it." Daniel jumps to his feet and slams his head on the underside of the stairs.

"Oh, shit!" April shouts. That did not sound good. She jumps to her feet, careful to avoid hitting her head too, and grabs Daniel by both elbows. "Are you alright?!"

He says he's fine, but he leans too heavily on April for her to believe it. "Sit," she insists, and helps him to the ground. Selfishly, she's a little relieved she is taking care of him, for once, and not the other way around. She also takes a brief moment to enjoy Alice flopping on the floor like a beached whale (a very in-shape, lovely beached whale in a truly fabulous blouse and a tight skirt) as she tries to stand.

See? April says to herself. *A pencil skirt may be sexy, but it's very impractical during a tornado warning.*

"I've got it," April says, crawling over Daniel's legs and Alice's ass (which is in the air, since Alice has made it to all fours). "Who's here?"

"My niece," Alice answers. April is out of the closet and rushing to the front door.

April sees Mimi standing in the torrential downpour outside. Well, downpour isn't even the right term. It's like a side-pour. Even standing under the awning, Mimi is getting pounded by rain moving horizontally.

It takes both of them, April pulling and Mimi pushing, to get the heavy front door open. Then it takes them both, pushing with all their might, to close the door against the wind.

As April leads Mimi to the closet, the lights go out. Mimi uses the flashlight on her phone to shine the way to the crawl space.

April's heart sinks at what the flashlight reveals under the steps. Alice sits with her back to the doorway, arms wrapped around Daniel's neck, her hands in his hair. He lets out a low groan. April can just make out his face over Alice's shoulder.

"Well, this is awkward," announces Mimi as she slides down to sit next to her aunt.

Alice glances back at Mimi but doesn't remove her hands from Daniel's hair. "He hit his head. The bump's only the size of a quarter."

"Ow," says Daniel as Alice pushes on his injury. "If you're going to poke at my bump, at least don't insult its size."

Alice stops feeling through Daniel's hair and turns her body to face the candle, sitting shoulder to shoulder between Mimi and Daniel. "Alright," she says dryly, "it's a very adequately sized knot."

April hunches in the door, waiting for her fellow stowaways to move so she can take her former spot on the other side of Daniel. Instead of moving, the three closet occupants stare up at April.

"Maybe we should shut the door?" Mimi suggests as she shuffles closer to Alice, who shuffles closer to Daniel, who shuffles closer to the wall to make more room for April to sit at the end of the closet—closest to the door and furthest away from Daniel.

"Of course." April pulls the door shut and sits next to Mimi. "I'm April," she says as she offers a cold hand to the young woman next to her. "We met at the art . . ."

"I know who you are," says Mimi as she slides a wet hand into April's. "Everyone does. I'm Mimi."

Again, probably not offensive that everyone knows who April is?

April's right side becomes wet as the rain in Mimi's clothes seeps into hers. Alice lays her towel on top of her niece to keep her warm. Now April is getting chilled and there are no sweaters or towels or broad, dry man arms to keep her from shivering.

Freaking, biceps-blocking Alice Deeds. Right then, a thunderclap, loud enough to wake the dead, startles them all. Daniel makes a wincing sound from the involuntary jerk of his head. April barely makes out his silhouette at the end of the line. "You okay?" she calls across the distance.

"Fine," he says.

After a moment of only ragged breathing filling the space, Mimi touches the soft fabric underneath them. "Is this the blanket from my registry?"

"No," says Daniel, "You chose the other one."

"Oh, shoot. This one is very comfortable, even on a cement floor."

"It's $150," says April. She's not sure, but it sounds like an exasperated puff of air exits Daniel's body two people down from her. "That's your registry on the white table?" April asks Mimi even though she knows the answer.

"Yes," Mimi nods. "I followed the advice in your book. I tried to register for reasonable items."

"Thanks a lot," Daniel says from the corner.

"Yes, well, be careful to not follow all the advice in the book." April can't seem to stop herself from saying too much. Her sense of failure spills into the small space beneath the stairs. There's an awkward silence followed by a loud crash. The crash is terrifying but still somehow a relief to April, who needs a diversion from her insecurities.

Daniel tries to stand up in the corner, but Alice pulls him back down.

121

"You're not going anywhere. I'll see what happened." But it makes zero sense for Alice and her pencil skirt to crawl across Mimi and April to get to the door.

"I'll check." April stands before anyone can protest. She opens the door and peeks into the English antiques room. Everything looks fine here, but there's a sound of gushing water coming from somewhere that is definitely not fine.

She moves out a few feet from the stairs, just enough to peer into the American antiques room. The problem is obvious. She steps back into the closet. "Unless there has always been a tree growing through the roof of the back room, a tree has fallen through the roof of the back room."

"Oh shit," Daniel grumbles as he tries to get to his feet.

"Stay," say April and Alice at the same time.

"Are the sirens still going?" Alice asks.

"I don't think so," April replies.

With Mimi's help, Alice makes it to her feet. The ladies venture into the American room to assess the damage. A sturdy bureau has caught the weight of the tree limb and minimized some of the damage to other furniture pieces, but water still pours in from the ceiling.

April doesn't know where to begin to stop the leak, but Alice, as it turns out, is a bit of a badass. April reluctantly falls a little in love with her over the next few hours.

21

Clean Up on Aisle A-five

Alice Deeds is a doer and April has always had an affinity for women who jump into a situation and handle business. In true country-girl fashion, Alice kicks off her heels and proceeds to move furniture, wield a shop vac, and haul large pieces of tree—all while wearing her fancy blouse and skirt.

April and Mimi are happy to follow Alice's instructions, and so are all the other people who show up to help. April marvels at the number of community members who descend on Antic Witties with chain saws, and ladders, and lunch—really good lunch. Alice must know who to call; within a couple of hours, it almost looks like nothing out of the ordinary happened in the American antiques room today.

In fact, by the time April gets Daniel back from Dr. White's with an ice pack and a clean bill of health, the only sign anything unusual has transpired is a giant stack of wet firewood piled up outside.

April deposits Daniel on a couch in the break room and finds Alice emptying the shop vac in the alley while wearing her two-inch heels. "Goodness," says April as she steps into the alley. "You move fast."

"I could say the same for you," Alice responds.

April is stunned into silence for a moment. She grabs the other side of the vacuum and helps Alice tip it over to spill the water onto the concrete.

When she responds, April sets her tone to *not-defensive/not-your-enemy mode* as she replies, "I don't move fast, actually. I'm like the tortoise of crushes.

I've liked Evan since the first day of eighth grade."

Alice releases the vacuum and stands upright. "What was he like as a teen?" she asks.

"Charming, gregarious, hard to discern if his intentions were genuine or for adoration," April replies.

"So, the same as now," Alice says.

"Exactly."

Alice takes a deep breath and then, in a brief moment of letting go of her usual controlled demeanor, says, "He called me April twice this week during meetings."

"So my observation wasn't pointless!" April exclaims. "It's easy to happen. We both have "A" names. Both five letters."

April tries to explain away the uncomfortable situation, but Alice isn't buying it. "Both women Evan would like to sleep with," she adds.

And there it is.

"Okay," says April. "Can we do this? Can we just be totally honest with each other? I haven't been single in so long, I don't know how single women look out for each other while navigating dating."

"I'd like for us to be direct," says Alice. "Believe it or not, I'm not usually the type who will wait while someone beats around the bush."

Uh, yeah, that's not hard for April to believe. "Alright," she begins, "adult me is sorry Evan said my name while talking to you. That's awful. You deserve better, and I will answer any question you want to ask me about him. Thirteen-year-old me can't believe Evan Treks said my name while staring at a gorgeous woman, with an impeccable taste in clothing, who has the super power of erasing a giant mess in a couple of hours."

Alice almost smiles. April is certain she sees a twitch at the corners of her perfectly lined lips.

"I do have the ability to clean up a big mess for someone else. That's basically my job. But, Daniel is easy to call in favors for. Because he does so much for others, people want to help him. So, did you sleep with him or what?"

"No!" sputters April. "We danced, but then he asked me to work for him.

So I just came by to tell him I don't want to work for him, but then the tornado hit. We got trapped. And now here we are."

"Alright," Alice finally cracks a smile, "but I was asking if you've slept with Evan, not Daniel."

"Oh," April's cheeks flush. "No."

"Did he try?"

April considers this. "Not really. We kissed, but if it makes you feel better at all, I made a total ass out of myself when I ran into him and his date at The Diner the next day."

Alice nods. "I heard about that date. Nothing is secret in a small town." She shows another tiny crack in her no-nonsense facade when she opens her mouth to speak, stops herself, and closes her mouth into a hard line. April can interpret this grimace; there are some things you don't ask, because you don't want the answer.

Alice switches gears. "Do you know the name of the woman he was with?"

"No," responds April.

"It's probably Amber," says Alice.

"Oh," April responds, "I'm not sure. I didn't recognize her."

Alice shakes her head. "I'm joking."

It takes April a second to get it. "Of course you are! Amber!!! The "A" name with five letters club!" April is definitely too over zealous about this bonding moment. "Oh my god, can we please rewind? You had the perfect callback and I've screwed it all up."

"The moment has passed," Alice says. She picks up the vacuum and makes her way to the back door of the shop.

"Oh, but isn't it so hard to tell sometimes." April says. It's not a question.

Alice turns around. "Evan isn't mine. He's never claimed me as his either. And I probably wouldn't want him if I could have him all to myself."

"I understand," says April. And she does.

"Since the 8th grade?!" Alice looks skeptical. "That's an awfully long time to have a crush." Alice disappears into the store.

The water has receded entirely from where it almost covered the wheel of the car a few hours ago. The cement is barely wet. Trashcans all up and down the alley are displaced; their contents strewn about. A Burger Barn cup has flown up to the landing of a fire escape on the building across the alley. April takes a moment to appreciate that the storm wasn't worse. She's known tornadoes to be unforgiving beasts.

As she turns to head inside, she takes in the mural on the back of Antic Witties. Daniel's mural. It's an eternal spring—bluebonnets in a field. Layered on top of the flowers are the words, *Everything Old is New Again*.

April finds Daniel sitting on the couch in the break room. There's a large farmhouse table, a hutch against the wall, a retro pink fridge, and a cozy corner with a couch and overstuffed chair. "I didn't take you for a pink fridge kind of guy," she says.

"Well, it wouldn't be the first time you're wrong about me." Daniel watches April as she moves across the room and sits in the chair near him.

April grabs the ice pack off the coffee table and adjusts it on the back of the couch so Daniel can tilt his head back to rest on the ice.

The gesture feels too familiar for a would-be boss and potential employee hanging out in the lounge. Well, maybe not the gesture itself so much as the fact it's performed in silence.

Silence is reserved for two people who are very comfortable with each other, or two people who are very uncomfortable with each other. April alternately believes she and Daniel are the former and then the latter.

"I appreciate the offer, but I don't need a job for the holidays." April sits back in her chair to get distance from Daniel.

He keeps his head tilted back on the ice pack but rolls his chin toward her. "I know you don't need it. I thought maybe . . ." Daniel stops himself. "It's no problem. I hope I didn't offend you by asking."

"No, of course not," April is quick to . . . well, lie. She's lying. Daniel briefly tries to read her expression, but he backs off and looks toward the ceiling.

April stares at the vanilla candle still burning but now sitting on the coffee table in front of them. "I'm sorry it took me so damn long to realize you were saying "hail". I was just flustered."

Daniel waves off her apology. "When was the last time you took shelter during a tornado?"

April relaxes further into the fluffy chair. "Freshman year. Remember how they would put us all in the basement of the high school?"

"Yes, on our knees, foreheads on the ground, hands laced on the back of our heads. It was painful." Daniel stands carefully and heads over to the hutch. He opens it to reveal a fancy bottle of bourbon. He holds it up and raises his eyebrows to say, "You want this?"

"Sure," April says. "Bourbon after a storm is a good tradition."

Daniel heads to the retro fridge for ice. "I remember that storm you're talking about in high school. I was a senior. When I got home, our trampoline was in the neighbors' yard. Totally undamaged, but it somehow jumped the fence we shared and ended up in their backyard. We never got it back. The neighbor kids loved it." Daniel pours a small amount of liquor into two glasses of ice and hands one to April.

"To the gift of the storm," April says as she clinks her glass against Daniel's.

He smiles. "The gift of the storm," he repeats. He sits on the couch as they both sip their drinks. "Even the other night at the fundraiser," he continues the thought, "it's awful the Carvers got sick, but I enjoyed getting to watch you host."

April can hear Dr. Novacheck in her head. She's supposed to accept compliments. "That's nice of you to say," April nods, "but you're a real asshole for not caring about the Carvers." Yes, okay. She accepted the compliment with humor. So what? She takes a sip as Daniel laughs.

She feels . . . it takes her a second to put a word to the sensation . . . comfortable. She feels comfortable. The surge of stress has passed and now she's in a cozy chair in a warm room, sipping smooth bourbon with no sense of urgency.

Nowhere to be except here.

22

Runnin' Down the Moon

The December before our wedding, Morgan and I drove through the New Mexico desert on Christmas Eve Eve at 2 a.m. We were trying to get home to surprise my parents for Christmas. The two-lane highway curved around and suddenly this monster of a moon hung low in the sky between two mountains dead ahead of us.

It looked like a painting. I'd never seen the moon look so big. "Watchin' the Wheels" by John Lennon played on the radio. There was nothing else, just us and the moon and the music.

We were in awe. Could real life really be so magical?

At the same time I understood what a privilege it was to be there with Morgan in that moment, I also felt a sadness tugging at my heart. This once in a lifetime moment was already escaping my grasp.

At first it looked like, if we could just drive fast enough, we'd run into the moon ahead of us. But the more we moved forward, the more the moon inched further into the sky. We'd never be able to catch it.

Excerpt from *Great Expectations* by April Townsend

It's 4:30 p.m. Sixty-eight presents wrapped today and April sits at the table in the wrapping/break room, unable to make herself stand. Daniel comes in looking equally exhausted and pats her shoulder.

"Are you okay?"

"I can't move," April replies.

Two weeks on the job, and despite Lilly's doubts, April's gift wrapping skills are receiving accolades. Sure, how-to videos online helped some—okay, they helped a lot, but April deserves credit for studying for the job.

"I've got something for that." Daniel pulls out the familiar bottle of bourbon from the hutch. They don't do this every day, just the ones that are extra busy.

As he retrieves ice from the freezer and pours two generous portions, April uses every ounce of her will to move from her seat at the long table to her fluffy chair. Daniel sets one glass in front of her while he holds his up in a toast.

"To my favorite wrapper."

They clink glasses. April sits back, enjoying a long, cold sip.

"I hope you don't mind the work much." Daniel falls onto the couch.

She doesn't. April's glad she took the job. The day goes quickly, and it's satisfying to have work that's both methodical and creative. Each gift wrap has a definitive beginning, middle, and end. The end always ties up in a neat little bow. That doesn't happen enough in life.

Plus, this job offers the benefit of permanent procrastination from making any progress on her house or her life.

April rolls her neck as she says, "I don't mind it, but today was a little ridiculous."

"Should I hire someone to help?" Daniel asks.

"No, I'm okay."

April enjoys binge listening to romance novels in her earbuds all day. A coworker might want to do something awful—like talk.

Talking with Daniel is different. He's willing to pretend he's interested in hearing the synopsis of whatever story she's been listening to that day. Somewhere deep down, April knows no one is actually interested in hearing someone else's synopsis of a book (it's almost as bad as hearing about someone else's dream), but Daniel humors her.

Last week, April was in a love-hate relationship with a novel about a football player falling for a small-town librarian. This week, she's giving updates on a holiday themed romance.

"Alright," says Daniel. "what happened with the couple who own the pine tree farm?"

"They don't own the farm," April corrects him. "He, Nicholas, owns the farm. And she, Noelle, has lost her job in the big city and returned to her small Christmas-themed town."

Daniel sits back in his chair, a wide smile on his face. "Nick and Noelle. What a coincidence their names fit the season."

April enjoys making him smile. "Don't ruin it for me," she cautions him.

"Hey, I'm not judging. My mom loves romance novels. I used to sneak into her room and look at the covers of her books."

"How did that work out for you?"

"Terribly. Big, buff dudes with their shirts ripped open. I assumed that's what women wanted."

"We do."

"Well, shit. Then I gotta hit the gym."

April laughs as her eyes wander to the biceps lifting Daniel's drink to his mouth. Moving furniture all day has its advantages.

"I finally got Mom to download the audio app from the library. What's the name of this Christmas romance?" Daniel asks.

April pauses. "Well, I wouldn't recommend this book to your mom."

"No?"

"No." April says this with finality, hoping to end this topic of conversation. No such luck.

Daniel's eyebrows raise in joyful intrigue. "I mean, all these books have some sexy stuff to them, right? That's part of the point."

"Not like this." April adjusts awkwardly in her seat. "I was about nine hours into it when the book turned from PG to porn with zero warning."

"What?!" Daniel's eyes water as the bourbon burns down the back of his throat.

"That is all I'm going to say about it," April insists. "I had to stop listening."

"Not your thing, then? Not into holiday porn?" Daniel asks.

"Not like that. Not out of nowhere while I'm at work."

Daniel's cheeks hurt from holding up his smile. He's dying for specifics, but April is the color of ketchup, so he backs off. "Okay. Just tell me the name of the book because I know someone who's REALLY into the holidays and I believe, as a good friend, I should share the title with this person I know."

April picks up her phone and shares the book info from her audio app to Daniel's number. "I can't bring myself to say it out loud," she says as she hits send.

Daniel holds his phone in anticipation. When the text comes through, he reads the title out loud. *"Love Under the Mistertoe".* Daniel looks to April. "That title didn't give you any hints as to the nature of the book?"

"In my defense," she laughs, "I read it as *Mistletoe*. I didn't notice the twist until I was already invested in the story." She brings her cool hands up to the sides of her scorching face. "Can we please talk about anything else?"

"Of course," says Daniel. "So, after this book went . . . south, and let's be honest, I would be disappointed if a romance novel about Mister Toe didn't go south . . . although you'd expect the North Pole to pop up somewhere in there . . . "

April cuts him off. "Stop it." Her laughter makes it sound as though she doesn't actually mean the words, but Daniel takes her command at face value.

"Okay." Daniel sits back. "What did you listen to after the rated X story?"

April attempts to cool off with the condensation rolling down her glass. She puts her head back and holds the icy drink to her throat. "I got through a whole podcast series about women betrayed by these men they trusted."

"So the opposite of Santa porn?"

"You gotta have balance," says April.

Daniel downs the last mouthful of his bourbon. "Do you feel like Morgan betrayed you?"

Man, sometimes his directness is jarring.

"Not like that," April answers. "Not while we were married anyway. These women, their whole romance wasn't real. Everything they thought about their love story was fake. Or, I mean, I don't know. Who am I to talk?"

Daniel can't keep watching little beads of water roll off April's tumbler, down her neck and under the collar of her shirt. He stands and reaches for her glass. "Refill?"

"Sure."

He crosses back to the bourbon. "What do you mean when you say, 'Who am I to talk?'" he asks.

"I mean, what do I know?" April takes off her boots and pulls her feet close to her in the chair. "I say my story isn't like those women who were living a lie, but I was kind of living a lie. I mean, I believed I was telling the truth when I wrote the book, but I didn't have all the facts."

Daniel defends April's integrity. "What facts are we talking about? Do you mean you have to know how something ends to determine if it's real? Because I don't think that's fair. We don't know how this conversation is going to end, but we can still be sure it's really happening." Daniel stands in front of April with her drink in his hand.

"I'm not sure what I mean. I don't want to argue about it." April puts her feet back in her shoes.

"No," Daniel backs off. His voice softens. "No. I'm sorry if it sounded that way. I'm not arguing. I'm just trying to figure it out with you. I don't have the answers either." He sits.

April takes a breath and a sip. "When I was trying to sort this out with my therapist, she asked me if a love story is still a love story even after it ends—even if the love eventually ends."

Daniel doesn't respond right away. The pause makes April wish she'd kept that information to herself.

When he finally speaks, he sounds so certain. "It is, right?"

"I don't know. You think it is, I guess," April answers.

"For sure. I was married to my high school sweetheart for five years."

Hearing Daniel talk about his first marriage simultaneously makes April relieved that Daniel also has a history of divorce and makes her feel something much more unpleasant, too.

"We grew apart by age 24," he continues. "It was an absolute, not meant to last, disaster of an ending. But were we in love at 18? Were we in love while we made out under the bleachers? Were we in love when we got married? Madly. Just couldn't think straight in love. And it was so damn fun. And of

132

course, our parents didn't understand. Of course, no one believed we would last. I mean, the writing was on the wall. But we weren't worried about the wall. We were runnin' down the moon, you know?"

"Runnin' down the moon?" April asks.

"It's something my grandmother used to say," Daniel shrugs, "mostly when she was describing my aunt Sarah who was married five different times."

"Five times? Did she ever find true love?"

"Yes." Daniel smiles. "Five different times."

April smiles too. She's just tipsy enough to seek satisfaction for her morbid curiosity. "Tell me about your marriage."

Daniel nods. "Right out of high school to Laura Faulkner."

"The twirler," April says.

"Yep."

"That one trick she did with the fire," April's gestures faintly resemble twirling and throwing a baton. "And the leg." Her arm draws a circle in the air.

"I know," says Daniel in a grave tone. "Believe me, I know. Nothing's hotter to a seventeen-year-old boy than a girl playing with fire."

April's not proud of it, but she feels jealous. Jealous of the teenage Laura with the flexible legs and the fire in her hands.

April wonders if Laura knows Daniel still talks with passion in his voice when he remembers their years together. She wonders if Laura knows Daniel can still emphatically say he loved her.

She wonders how Morgan would describe their first years together now. What does he tell his new girlfriend about his time with April?

"You ever talk to her?" April asks.

"No. I mean, on social media, we have mutual friends. She's been married for fifteen years or something now and has four kids."

"Wow."

"Yep. Do you and Morgan talk?"

"Uh . . . no. Except for what I told you about him dating someone. But he didn't tell me himself. He told my sister to tell me."

Daniel's face turns serious. "You don't deserve that. I'm sorry."

133

The sincerity of Daniel's response causes April's eyes to sting. His kindness threatens to whip up some emotions April doesn't want whipped.

"Do you still love him?" Daniel asks.

April panics at the question. She doesn't answer at first.

"You don't have to answer that," Daniel offers.

"I don't think I can answer," April says. "I don't know. I'm aware of all these reasons it's better we're not together but . . . I still get nauseous thinking of him with someone else."

Daniel says it before he has a chance to back out, "Have you been with anyone since Morgan?" April's face betrays her once again. It's a curse to flush so easily.

"Yes," she says.

Daniel nods as though to reassure her. Yep, it's perfectly normal to sleep with other people after you get divorced. But he nods a little too much for a little too long to convince April or himself that he wants to hear anymore.

"Do you want me to elaborate?" April smiles.

"Not really. No," he answers.

"I'll just say this, it's like I felt compelled to get it over with. Like checking off a post-divorce to-do list."

Daniel nods. Once. He makes sure he just nods once. "Did it help? Checking off that box?"

"It didn't do what I hoped it would."

"What's that?"

April sips her drink, then brings her arm down on the armrest closest to Daniel. "Make me forget how much fucking pain I was in."

Daniel feels a pull in his chest. April deserves the kind of sex that's so good it makes her forget everything else in the world. He'd like to volunteer to help with that, but it's not a good idea.

Still . . .

Daniel reaches forward and runs his index finger down the condensation on the side of April's glass until his finger meets her hand where it grasps the drink. A tiny, cold drop of water, displaced by Daniel's interference, runs over April's knuckles. Daniel's finger traces the trail of water, moving over the bend of April's fingers until it lingers on her empty ring finger.

They both startle when the door chime rings. Bourbon spills over the top of April's glass and runs down her hand.

"Shit," says Daniel as he laughs. "I forgot the door." He stands as April licks the trail of bourbon from her fingers. When she catches Daniel's eye, he's frozen—staring at her as she tastes the ring finger he just touched.

He's not laughing anymore. The smile is there, but the look in his eyes is not just friendly . . . not just friendly at all.

23

Please Don't Be Nice

Daniel does end up hiring an additional wrapper. Mimi got recruited to help one morning after coming in to check on her registry. At the time, April had twenty candles to wrap for a customer who stopped in on her way from Houston to Dallas. Daniel attempted to help April, but he had customers to attend to.

Mimi has a natural flare for wrapping gifts. She picked up the register quickly too. In fact, she taught April the basics so April can cover the front when Daniel makes deliveries while Mimi is on her break.

April is surprised how much she enjoys having Mimi around.

She is also surprised how much she enjoys working at the antique store.

She is triple surprised how much Daniel has avoided her since the evening he fingered her fingers. Wait. No. That phrasing sounds quite a bit more risque than the actual encounter.

But the actual encounter was charged. April is sure of that. She's been out of the game for a while, but there was no mistaking Daniel's look at the end of that exchange.

April thought about it all night that night. On her way to work the next morning, she was all nerves. Well, all nerves or all excitement; they can be interchangeable where romance is concerned.

But she didn't need to be nervous, as it turned out, or excited. That next day and every day since, Daniel has kept his distance from April.

He seems relieved to have Mimi in place. And, honestly, April is too. Mimi works hard, and she has a nice neutral effect. There's no risk of a sexually charged encounter with Mimi around. That may sound like an insult, but April considers it a compliment under the current circumstances. Mimi provides a safe space for April to figure out she likes the work and not just the boss.

Evan and Daniel are both dangerous for April. Evan because he is not a serious distraction, and Daniel because he could be.

The logical part of April, the part that can only function when Evan or Daniel aren't nearby, knows a distraction from her heartache (as much as she might wish for it) isn't a substitute for the work she has to do.

It's like she has a pile of dishes in her sink—a stinking, filthy, overwhelming pile of dishes—and going out for the night might be a nice break from the mess, but those dishes will still be there when she gets back home. And they'll smell even worse.

That's the metaphor she uses to comfort herself over Daniel's standoffish behavior; she's got to wash the dishes anyway.

For the first time in her life, April discovers being on a schedule is good for her. A schedule eliminates some of the overwhelming decisions of life. It gives a context to work in. It means April isn't trying to create a life out of thin air. She's just trying to get through a work day broken up into three hours before lunch and four hours after.

There's less time to think.

Today is supposed to be April's day off because she taught her online class this morning, but Mimi needed a last-minute dress fitting, so April covers the register for the last few hours of the day.

Daniel seemed flustered when April showed up after lunch. He's been finding excuses to stay in the stockroom for the last two hours. It's slow up front, anyway. But there's a customer buying some small gifts, and April's phone starts ringing as she rings up the purchases.

She apologizes to the customer. She's in the habit of turning the ringer off on her way to work, but coming in on her day off throws her usual routine. She reaches under the counter to stop the noise and can't help but see the name of the caller lit up on her screen.

Morgan.

Shit.

Seeing his name on her screen used to be commonplace. In fact, it used to be that seeing his name elicited no reaction at all. Often, she'd mute his calls or ignore his texts, and then forget to respond later. But now, seeing his name brings wonder and terror. She's right back to feeling how she did the day he told her he wanted a divorce, like all her organs are in the wrong place.

Her hands shake as she rings up the purchases on the digital register. She hits the wrong thing twice and has to call Daniel up from the back room to fix her mistakes. April apologizes to the customer again as she attempts to verbally explain to Daniel what she's done wrong. She wants to avoid showing him, because she doesn't want him to see her shaking hands.

But as the customer's patience starts to waiver, Daniel says, "Can you just show me what you did?"

April relents. She lifts a visibly vibrating hand to point out the buttons on the screen. Daniel looks from her wavering fingers to her face. She avoids eye contact. Daniel puts a reassuring hand on April's back. His shoulders soften. "I've got it. Thanks. Why don't you take your break."

It's not time for her break.

April grabs her phone, wishes the woman well, and heads to the alley. An excruciating thirty seconds of waiting finally ends with a voicemail notification. What the hell is he calling for? He never makes phone calls. He ended their marriage by text, for god's sake.

She leans against the bluebonnet mural, trying to steady her legs as Morgan's voice fills her ear for the first time in months. The message is short and awkward.

He says his name, as though April might not know the sound of his voice. He says Lilly told him he needed to call. He says he's getting married.

"I heard you moved to Texas," he says. "That's wild. Hope it's a fun adventure."

That's it. Over a decade of marriage.

Hope it's a fun adventure.

When Morgan told April he wanted a divorce, that there was no other choice left for him, that he was done, that counseling would not fix their marriage, that nothing could fix it, he claimed he longed to be alone. He ached to buy that stupid camper and drive to the middle of nowhere and just be by himself to figure out who he was.

Well, that didn't even last a year—if it was ever true to begin with. Now he has someone. They're getting married. April, who hadn't wanted to get a divorce or be alone, has, in fact, made it longer as a single person than her husband, who purported to be dying for solitude.

Why would he marry someone after knowing her for a few months?!

Oh god. Oh shit. If she's pregnant . . .

Daniel opens the alley door from the shop. April speaks before he can. "Don't be nice to me."

"Okay." Daniel doesn't hesitate to respond.

"I'm fine. But if you're nice, I might lose it."

"Got it." Daniel nods and falls silent as he stands in the doorway.

April takes a breath. "Sorry I . . ."

"Fuck you," Daniel says.

April's head whips up in surprise. Daniel meets her shocked expression with a small smile.

"You take direction well," she squeaks.

"Like hell I do, you . . . dick. Just come back to work whenever the hell you feel like it." Daniel turns to head inside; the door slams behind him for emphasis.

Something comes out of April's lungs sounding a lot like laughter. When her hand covers her mouth, she's surprised to find the corners of her lips turned up.

It's a risk to say "fuck you" to someone who is upset, particularly to an employee who is upset. Also, a risk to call them a "dick".

And April is . . . flattered.

Daniel doesn't handle her like she is one of his delicate antiques—requiring a gentle touch. He treats her like she's the bureau that held up the tree branch. Like she's built strong. Like she can hold a shit ton of weight without breaking.

And he trusts her sense of humor. That might be the nicest compliment she's had in a long time.

April's confidence took a beating this last year. Maybe that's what she loathes most about this whole mess. She can't trust herself anymore. She can't even trust her gut, which is currently in her chest, or her heart, which is currently cowering in the pit of her stomach. She does not want to feel this way.

Fuck the dirty dishes in her metaphorical sink (and honestly, in her literal sink too)! She'll take any distraction. She marches back into the store, prepared to ask Daniel if it's too early for a bourbon, but the store has three customers. Three friends who have money and time.

April turns it on, that part of her who is the host. Daniel sees it happen just like he saw it the night of the fundraiser. She transforms and the customers are just as enamored with her as Daniel was that night backstage.

The friends spend the next two hours shopping. While April handles it all with ease, Daniel is slowly coming undone. He's clumsy and aloof. It annoys April. If she's the one who's upset and she can pull herself together, what's his problem?

Maybe he's second guessing calling her a dick. Like, saying "fuck you" to someone who is on the verge of an emotional breakdown is one thing, but calling that person a "dick" might be a step too far.

The ladies spend over $2500. Still, Daniel doesn't crack a smile. He brings in the sandwich board from outside, even though it's only 4:45 p.m. "We should close early. That was a good sale. We can just go ahead and close," he rushes.

"Oh, I still have some presents to wrap . . ."

"It can wait until tomorrow," Daniel interrupts.

"Daniel, I'm fine to close," April says. "I'd rather finish or I'll start off behind tomorrow."

"I'm sorry," he says. "I planned to leave a few minutes early. I'd talked to Mimi about it." Daniel won't make eye contact with April.

"That's fine," April assures him. "I can close up."

"I can change my plans."

"It is fine. I am fine. I promise." April tries to sound reassuring without a hint of annoyance that he's being so awkward while she's keeping her shit together so beautifully.

"Ok." He clearly wants to say more, but he stops himself and grabs his keys from under the counter instead. "Thanks for working today."

"That's what you pay me for," April responds.

Daniel finally looks her in the eyes. "You sure you're okay?"

"Yes," she answers. And she's surprised how certain she sounds.

"I'll see you tomorrow," he says as he exits.

April attempts to wrap the remaining gifts, using every ounce of her will to put Morgan out of her mind. She's not excelling at either effort. She's thankful when the bells on the front door interrupt her tasks. Even though it's after closing time, she's willing to let a customer look around. She needs a distraction.

As she comes to the front of the store, April finds an attractive woman in form fitting jeans and high heels approaching the counter. The woman seems surprised to see her.

"Hi. Is Danny here?" she asks.

Why does April's stomach churn at the word "Danny"?

"No, you just missed him."

"Oh," the woman looks sheepish, almost apologetic. "Do you happen to know where he was going?"

"No, I'm sorry. He just said he needed to leave a little early." April omits the fact that she wouldn't tell a stranger where her boss was, even if she knew.

"Okay, thank you." The woman hesitates as though she's not sure if she should say more, then she turns to leave.

A voice in April's head warns her not to ask, but the words are already leaving her mouth, "Can I help you with something?"

The woman stops and turns around. "This will sound strange, but do you know a restaurant around here where the chef is Australian?"

"Buckney's," replies April.

"Buckney's!" the woman says. "Thank you." She pulls out her phone to look up directions to Buckney's.

April, don't ask questions you don't want answers to . . . "Are you supposed to meet Daniel there?" She tries to sound casual.

"Yes, and I dropped my personal phone and destroyed it. I've got my work phone, but it doesn't have Danny's number or any of our messages."

Any of our messages.

April tries to recall how many times she's seen Daniel pick up his phone over the last couple of weeks.

"Oh, that's too bad," April says outwardly. But inwardly her brain takes off: *Oh, this feels real shitty and I'm ready to either cry or punch this woman in her beautiful fucking face even though she seems to be nice and I don't know how to punch and perhaps I'll wait until the next time I see Daniel and punch him in his beautiful fucking face for cussing me out today and making me like him even more even though he ignored me after fingering my fingers weeks ago and dancing with me and then offering me a shitty job which isn't really shitty but now probably will be because I've got (possibly displaced) anger toward my boss who has a date tonight.*

The woman continues, "I just thought I'd come early and pop in here. Try to catch him."

"Well, I'm sorry you missed him," April smiles.

"That's okay. I can find him now. You've been very helpful. Thank you."

"Sure," says April. "Anytime."

The woman leaves. April stands frozen. Daniel has a date tonight. That woman is Daniel's date. And they've been messaging for weeks.

For the second time today, April is spiraling downward. This time, Daniel isn't here to cuss her out of it. This time, he's the problem.

24

Drive

At 8:30 p.m., there's a knock on April's door. She's halfway through a cheeseburger and a pile of fries from Burger Barn, which is a delicious (but not distracting enough) distraction.

She tries to keep herself from hoping it's Daniel at the door. April has never been a fan of people stopping by unannounced, but if it's the right person . . .

She pulls the door open to find Evan.

He holds up a new car key. "Wanna go for a ride?" Past Evan and his hypnotic new key, April sees a navy blue BMW with the tags still on.

"Sure. Why not." The "why not" is meant to convince herself.

Evan catches the hesitance. "Well, don't hold back your enthusiasm on my account."

April shakes her head to recalibrate. "I'm sorry. I'm dying to go for a ride in your new convertible."

"That's better," Evan smiles. And when Evan smiles, even miserly old men get an involuntary pull in their midsection. As April grabs her purse, she questions whether she has the good sense to say no to Evan when he asks for something, especially tonight.

April leaves her phone on the counter. She wants to drive with loud music blaring and wind hitting her face so furiously she can hardly breathe. She does not want an ankle monitor on the floorboard by her feet, which is what

143

her phone would be.

Evan is pretty damn cute as he sings along to "I Drove All Night" at April's request. Well, April requested the song, not necessarily the singing. The smell of the new car makes Evan even more attractive. April considers for a moment whether one can get drunk off of new-car scent, because she feels buzzed.

It could be the chilly wind, or Evan speeding down Farm to Market 1203, or Cyndi Lauper's voice, but April is allowing herself to be carried away from new fiancés, and new dates at Buckneye's, and any other stories that make her stuck in a sad and lonely place.

Out of the dark, an old gas station appears. Evan pulls into the lot and parks under the neon sign. It's difficult to tell if it's even open, but Evan seems to know the place. He fist bumps the guy behind the counter when they walk in. April doesn't like the glance the guy gives her. He's almost smirking like, "So you're tonight's girl".

Evan buys a six-pack of mixed imported beers. He and the attendant chat about some featured beer of the week. April wouldn't have taken this attendant as the kind of dude who bothers with imported featured beers of the week, but she would have been wrong.

Evan explains in the car on the way back to town; that gas station is a destination beer spot. People drive from miles around to check out the new weekly selections. Plus, the station does a mix and match, which is unusual for a pit stop.

Then Evan asks if April wants to come back to his place to try the beers.

She considers it for a moment. "How many women have you taken to that gas station?"

Evan glances at her, then back to the road ahead. "I'll take you home, Townsend," he says. April wonders if that's supposed to be a punishment for asking a question that's off limits. Evan wants to be the present moment only. Questions are instruments of the future.

April closes her eyes and leans into the headrest. The familiar Rolling Stones opening to "(I Can't Get No) Satisfaction" blares over the car speakers. While her hair whips in her face, April decides she isn't sorry for asking. She spent the last few years of her marriage never asking the questions she didn't want the answers to. Her lack of inquisitiveness didn't change the outcome. It may have prolonged the inevitable. But it didn't prevent it.

Either now, before she sleeps with Evan, or later, after she sleeps with him, she'll have to confront the fact she's not special to him. Not in the long run. He's not tailoring his efforts to fit her. He's a one-size-fits-all kind of dater.

"The truth is," she shouts over the wind and the music, "I'm not into mixing and matching beers. Sometimes I wish I was, but I don't think I am."

Evan smiles. "I thought that might be the case, but I want you to know you're worth getting rejected for. I'd always regret it if I didn't ask."

While she reminds her insides to settle down, April can't help but to reciprocate Evan's smile. Being wanted by Evan is flattering, even if she knows she's not the only beverage on the bar.

"I do appreciate the offer," she says.

After a pause, Evan says, "You know, Daniel is a good guy."

April isn't sure if Evan is perceptive or if everyone in town assumes she and Daniel are interested in each other. Small town, two single people working together has to have started some rumors.

"Nothing is happening with me and Daniel."

"No?"

"No. He's actually on a date tonight at Buckneye's."

"Oh good, so you already know." Evan sounds relieved.

"You knew he was on a date?"

"Yes, I was drinking at the bar, with a beautiful woman, by the way. And when I saw Daniel with someone that wasn't you, I just wanted to be sure you were okay."

April tries to read Evan's face for a hint of his usual tricks, but he seems sincere. "Really?" she has to ask.

"Yes. Listen, I was married for ten years." This is news to April. "She broke my heart. After that, I swore I was going to have all the fun I wouldn't have had if we'd stayed married, but I'm not an asshole. You and I go way back. I care about you."

April isn't sure how to respond. So she says something wild. "My ex called me today to tell me he's getting married." April could not have predicted that Evan, of all people, would be the one she'd tell first. She's nervous to see if this was a mistake.

He seems to take the information in stride. He turns down the music. "Was he cheating on you?"

"No. I don't think so. He met this woman while living out of his van in the desert post-divorce."

Daniel looks surprised by this. "Was she like . . . wandering in the desert?" he asks. "Are there a lot of single ladies hanging out on the sand dunes?"

April hadn't thought of it. How the hell did Morgan meet someone in the desert?

"Should I vacation in Mojave?" Evan asks.

"Maybe," says April. "Palm Desert gone wild."

"Come for the 120 degree heat. Stay for the hot chicks." Evan looks in April's direction. Her mouth is smiling at his joke, but her eyes aren't. He reaches over to cover her hand in his. "My heart's not broken anymore," he says. "It's not the same as it was, but it's not broken."

"How long did it take?" asks April.

"A little while," he says. "Now let's go get you a drink."

Evan brings April home thirty minutes later with a large cherry limeade from the gas station on 7th Ave. That station was the most popular haunt of high schoolers back in the day. It still has the best sodas.

Alone inside her house, April tries to avoid rushing to her phone, but she pretty much rushes to her phone. It's 10:30 p.m. now. She has two missed calls from Lilly and a text from Demmy.

Demmy: Are you dragging 7th with Evan?

April thought news traveled fast in Cleo when she was younger. With cell phones now, it travels in real time.

She's disappointed there's no text from Daniel. That's the truth of it. But she's not sure if she wants a text from Daniel to distract from the Morgan situation, or if she wants a text from Daniel because she wants Daniel.

One thought she had in Evan's car, one thing that made her turn him down, was the thought she might come home to a message from Daniel. And, somehow, hearing from Daniel after sleeping with Evan, would make her feel like she'd let Daniel down. Which makes no sense, of course, because Daniel is not worried about letting April down. He's too busy on his damn date to even think about April, much less text her.

So no. There's no reward for stepping back from the edge of the abyss tonight, except, of course, being safe from the danger of falling into the abyss.

April wishes she wasn't so out of sorts. Surely she's too old to have her feelings easily moved by the action or inaction of men. Instead, she's still the nine-year-old kid getting crushed by the boys she likes.

It occurs to her though, while she's brushing her teeth, she ought to be at least a little proud of herself for not going down the rabbit hole of Evan tonight. She didn't clear her sink of any dishes, but she didn't add to them either.

It would have been so easy to make an impulsive move to try to thwart the bad news of the day, but April stayed levelheaded. It feels like she won back a little trust in herself this evening.

Even if her feelings rise and fall at the mercy of a message from a man, her actions belong solely to her.

25

Asses to Asses, Crush to Crush

April texts Lilly in the morning to assure her sister she's dealing with the news from Morgan as best she can. That means keeping busy.

She sets up a lunch date with Demmy via text before heading into Antic Witties thirty minutes before they open. It's not like she was sleeping anyway. The one time she did nod off, she dreamed the woman who came in to Antic Witties to find Daniel was pregnant with Morgan's baby—then the baby was born and it had a tiny Evan face.

It will just be April and Mimi this morning, which will hopefully give April a chance to figure out how to deal with Daniel when he comes in after lunch.

The security alarm is already shut off when she keys into the store. Mimi must be around here somewhere. April heads into the break room to make a pot of coffee per her usual routine, but it's already brewing. She opens the fridge to get the half and half, but there isn't any in the door. She squats down to rummage through the shelves.

"Looking for this?" Daniel's voice from the doorway startles the shit out of April as she falls backward onto her ass. Her tailbone hits the hard floor in just the wrong way, creating a shock of pain that surges up her body and into her throat. She rocks back and forth for a moment, trying to breathe through the pain and pressing her lips together to avoid howling.

Daniel can't see any of this through the open fridge door, which blocks his view. He just hears silence.

"You okay?"

"Fine," April spits out. But she sounds pissed. And Daniel assumes . . .

"Listen, I'm sorry Brittany came here looking for me."

Brittany? Why did he have to say her name? April most definitely does not want to hear him say her name.

"It's fine." She can barely speak through the hurt.

"Really? Because you sound angry."

Dammit. April's eyes fill with tears. It's the same involuntary reaction she used to have as a kid when she injured herself. It's a self-inflicted addition of insult to injury. And now April IS angry.

"I don't care about your stupid date. I hurt myself when you startled me."

Daniel rushes to peer over the fridge door and down at April, who looks defiant even with tears streaking down her cheeks.

"Are you okay?" he asks.

"No." she says.

"What did you hurt?"

"My ass. Alright?! I hurt my ass!"

She's laughing by the time she says "ass" for the second time. Daniel gets behind April, looping his arms under her armpits to help her up. She's laughing so hard, she shakes against his body—which makes him laugh too.

It takes much longer than it should for Daniel to get April off the floor and onto her feet. The longer it takes, the longer it takes because they're laughing about the amount of time it's taking.

Finally, she is up, and they are settling down. Daniel takes a step back as he lets go of her.

"I'm sorry," he says, "about yesterday."

April wipes away tears. "You didn't do anything wrong."

"Are you sure?" he asks.

April shrugs. "It was just a hard day."

"Look," he walks to the table and gets a carton of half and half out of the grocery bag he set on the edge. He holds it up. "Let's restart." He crosses to the coffee hutch.

"I think we've tried that before," April says as she walks stiffly over to a

149

chair at the table, her tailbone still trying to recover.

Daniel pours April's coffee with a little cream, just the way she likes it. He sets it down in front of her, then heads back to the hutch and, under the safety of having his back to April, he says the thing he knows he shouldn't say.

"About a million people texted me last night to say they saw you and Evan dragging 7th in his new car."

April pegs Daniel with an incredulous look. Secretly, she notes (with a little flicker of satisfaction) that fielding a million texts during a date probably didn't bode well for the date. "Dragging 7th?" she says. "What are we, sixteen again? We were driving down 7th. And why would *a million* people text you about that?"

Daniel sits at the head of the table a few feet from April. "I don't know. Because we work together maybe. People want to know the gossip. They want to know what I know about you."

"And what do you tell them?"

"I tell them I don't know. Because you don't talk to me much about personal stuff."

"I don't talk to anyone about personal stuff."

"You talk to Evan, apparently."

"I don't talk to Evan about anything," she lies. And somehow, in the lying, April emphasizes the word "talk" and it comes across to Daniel as though she's implying she and Evan do things other than talking.

For a moment, Daniel has the wind knocked out of him.

He stands. April shakes her head in frustration. She doesn't mind Daniel being jealous, especially after the night she spent picturing him and . . . Brittany. But she doesn't mean to make him think she slept with Evan.

"That didn't come out right." April reaches for Daniel and catches his bicep. His muscles tighten under her touch and she loses her concentration. She smiles.

"What?" He sounds defensive.

"I forgot. I forgot what I was trying to say."

"You and Evan . . ."

"No! Nothing."

"Not even a kiss?" he asks.

April's smile fades. "I'm sorry," he says. "I have no right to ask that."

April answers him anyway. "Not last night."

Daniel's chest tightens. So they have kissed. This. This shitty feeling is exactly what he was trying to avoid the day he told April they should just be friends. He's thankful the front door chimes. "I'll get it," he says, pulling out of April's grasp.

"I'm sure it's just Mimi," April starts, but Daniel is already out of the room.

The business day continues as usual except that Daniel avoids being in the same room as April when he can help it. He's only in her presence when bringing purchases for her to wrap. Even Mimi notices his odd behavior. And he never explains to either of them why he's come in on his morning off.

At lunch, Demmy is very sympathetic about the situation with Morgan. She listens to April unload her entire thought process in a booth at The Diner. April makes a small, internal observation that she doesn't actually feel like talking about the situation with Morgan. But she'd rather talk about the situation with Morgan than try to dissect the situation going on across the street.

When April returns to Antic Witties after lunch, Daniel is upstairs rearranging the storage loft. April finds this location to be even more annoying than when he hides in the stockroom. Now, when it gets busy, she has to work the front of the store as he literally hangs over her.

He doesn't come down until 5 p.m. to close the register. In an effort to avoid being alone for the night, April invites Mimi for a drink as they walk out of the store. Daniel looks up from his work for the first time and orders them to wait.

He takes sixty dollars out of the register and holds it out to them. "Thank you for taking care of things down here today. You should go to dinner."

April stands frozen, but Mimi bounds up to the register and takes the cash. "Thank you!" she says. "You should come with us."

Daniel's eyes move to April. "I have work to do," he says. "Go have fun."

When April pulls into her driveway after a nice sushi dinner with Mimi, she sees a very familiar package on the front porch. It's wrapped in the same paper and ribbon she uses at the store, but this wrapping job isn't her work.

Suddenly, this giddy little flutter she hasn't felt in a very long time, passes through her.

She makes herself wait until she's gotten ready for bed. Then she sits on her blow up mattress in her pajamas and opens the gift. It's a vanilla lavender candle. There's a note written neatly on the tiny gift card:

I'm sorry I knocked you on your ass today.

And I'm sorry I was an ass.

Hope you are okay.

-Danny

(P.S. If this is too nice . . . fuck you.)

26

The One With the Elf

The Historical Society of Cleo is hosting a holiday party on the twelfth floor of the tallest building in town. They've been trying to get the Stamen Building restored for years. There's a bank on the bottom floor, but a lot of the upper floors are raw space.

Demmy, of course, serves on the preservation committee and she's asked April to help with the party. April realizes her entire social life revolves around Demmy's charity work. It's like two degrees of separation from being charitable herself. April is charitable-adjacent.

She brings her dress and heels to work. During their lunch hour, Mimi helps her with an updo of red flowers and a much better make-up job than April could do on her own. It's been just the two of them the last couple days. Daniel's been to the wholesale market in Dallas with Joel. Usually only Joel can go this time of year, but now Daniel has two capable employees to run the store while he shops for new inventory.

April can't stop wondering if Brittany is involved with the market—maybe Danny and Brit are spending their days and nights together right now. Mimi brought the idea up first. She heard from her waitress friend at Buckneye's that Daniel came in with a beautiful date. April filled in the name Brittany.

Mimi mentioned (and April thinks of it nonstop since) the possibility Daniel and Brittany might be connected through the market. That would explain why Daniel decided to attend at the last minute. This is a hypothesis

April could live without.

Attempting to focus on something else yesterday, April used the pay she received from teaching online and bought herself a new dress from the shop next door. It was supposed to cheer her up, but now she just feels guilty about spending the money.

Since she has to wait for the holiday party to start anyway, April volunteers to close the store tonight. As Mimi exits, Demmy comes in with a garment bag.

"Hello, Santa's Little Helper," she says.

April does not like the sound of this greeting. "What's in the bag?"

Demmy drops all pretense. "Hear me out . . ."

"No," says April.

"I haven't even said anything!"

"If that's an elf costume, I'm not wearing it." Demmy is kidding, of course. She doesn't really expect there to be an elf costume in the bag. That would be ridiculous. So . . . why isn't Demmy laughing?

"It's not a costume. It's a hand sewn designer dress . . . for an elf," Demmy says.

"Demmy!" April pleads.

"It's made by one of our board members. It's gorgeous . . . for an elf dress. I swear to you I was going to wear it myself, but it's too small."

"No one needs an elf at this party," April insists.

"It's tradition. Mrs. Jensen makes a costume every year for Santa and for an elf and they get auctioned off at the end of the night."

"I am not being auctioned off!"

"This isn't that kind of party. The costumes get auctioned off, not the people wearing them. You won't believe how much money these things raise for the Historical Society."

"Who's Santa?" April asks.

"Evan," says Demmy, "and he has to stuff a pillow under his belt and wear a beard. He's not afraid to look very goofy."

"That's not helping your case. I don't want to look goofy at a holiday party when I'm barely getting to know these people."

"No. You don't have to look goofy," Demmy says with desperation. "I'm trying to say that Evan does it even though he looks ridiculous. The elf costume is actually kind of fun."

"Definitely not helping your case." April moves to lock the front door.

"Please. Please. Please." Demmy begs.

"Why not ask Alice to do this?"

"I already did."

April groans, "So she's going to be laughing at me for being the sucker?"

"She won't be there. I think she avoids Evan when she can." Demmy unzips the garment bag. "At least see the thing before you say no." She pulls out the elf costume.

"Yes, it's very pretty," says April, "for an elf costume." She's not lying. It's made of a soft, dark-green velvet. It looks almost like a swing dress lined with white faux fur. And it has a little pointy hat to go with it.

April tries another tactic. "Mimi already fixed my hair. I bought a new dress."

Demmy has hope in her voice. She may have won this battle. "You can wear your hair like it is. Don't worry about the hat. And I'll pay you back for your dress. I'm desperate. Please."

"I don't want to be on display this time. I already did that for the last event."

"It's for a good cause," Demmy tries.

"A building?" says April. "It was a persuasive argument when it was 'for the children', but 'for the building' doesn't quite have the same pull."

Demmy shrugs. "It's history. Doesn't history matter? Plus, it's for me. And I'd owe you big time."

April closes her eyes. "And you'll pay for my dress?"

"Absolutely. Give me the receipt right now."

Fifteen minutes later, April is alone and finished closing down the shop. She heads into the bathroom (taking a glass of bourbon with her) to transform into an elf.

As elf costumes go, this one's well-made. April looks at herself (at least as much as she can see in the small bathroom mirror), takes a sip of her drink and says to no one, "I'm too old for this shit."

She pulls on the red knee-high nylons Demmy provided, slips into her high heels, and heads out of the bathroom . . . to find Daniel standing at the register. He must have come in through the alley door because she didn't hear the bell chime at the front. April considers turning tail and exiting out the back, but Daniel notices her before she can move.

He does a double take.

"I thought you were at the market," April says.

"I just got back. I have work to do."

"Who was there with you?" She can't help herself.

"Joel," Daniel says as he turns to fully face her. He leans back against the counter behind him . . . waiting.

"I'm an elf," April explains.

"Yes, I see that."

"I'm doing it for Demmy. I feel like a . . . dipshit," she says.

"You don't look like a dipshit," he says.

"Well, I feel like I look like a dipshit."

"Listen, I'm not an expert in dipshits, but I'm pretty sure they don't look like . . . that." The way Daniel says "that" as his eyes run up and down April's costume, it sounds almost as if he's implying April looks hot.

She doesn't know how to respond. One doesn't ask, "Are you implying that I look sexy in this elf costume?" Because if that is not what the other person is implying, then one definitely looks like a dipshit.

"Have you seen yourself?" Daniel treads carefully. He is, after all, her boss.

"Just in the bathroom mirror."

Daniel gestures for April to follow him into the English antiques room where there is a larger makeup mirror on top of a dresser. "Stay there," he says, as he adjusts the mirror to aim down. From her spot several feet from the dresser, April can see more of her outfit. It's shorter than she realized. And paired with the knee-high socks, this outfit could pass for a high-end, naughty-elf costume.

"Oh my god," April says. "Am I holiday porn? Am I in *Under the Mistertoe* territory?!"

156

Daniel is enjoying this entirely too much. "No. You are not rated X-mas. But I'd be lying if I said you weren't at least in PG-13 zone."

"It's not embarrassing?" April sort of half-asks, half-states as she looks at herself in the mirror. She means, of course, that as far as dressing as an elf goes (which is inherently embarrassing unless you are in a room full of other people dressed like elves), she looks alright. Even she has to admit she looks alright. Elves. Who knew?

"No," Daniel shakes his head. "You definitely do not have anything to be embarrassed about."

And he leaves it at that, because he fears he already said too much.

27

The One With the Elevator

It's not as bad as April worried it would be, but it's not good. Everyone wears fancy attire at this party. Fancy, conservative attire. And here's April being an elf—bordering on being a naughty elf.

Luckily, Evan is taking up most of the air in the room with his velour Santa costume and satin collar. And he doesn't look goofy, as Demmy promised. He looks like Stud Santa, only with an enormous belly and beard. Honestly, April has to wonder what this Mrs. Jensen is into. April might have an audio book she could recommend to her.

April insists on working the bar with Demmy. This way, she can hide half her outfit behind the bar top. Before the heavy hors d'oeuvres are to be served, the line at the bar is long.

Demmy looks up from pouring glasses of wine. "Oh, he made it."

April follows her gaze to see Daniel stepping off the elevator and looking around the room. As soon as he spots the long line of people in front of Demmy and April, he comes to help. He grabs a wine opener and starts working on a bottle of merlot.

"I thought you had to work," says Demmy. The knowing smirk she's sporting does not escape April's notice.

"I . . . yes, but I decided to take a break. See how you're doing," he responds.

Demmy knows what Daniel is doing, but she wonders if Daniel knows what Daniel is doing.

With the extra help, the line whittles down quickly. Demmy pours a glass of wine for herself as she steps from behind the bar to mingle.

"April," she says to her friend, "please consider a walk around the room so people actually see the outfit they're bidding on. You look good. Doesn't she look good?" Demmy looks to Daniel for help.

"She looks great," says Daniel. Yep, still sticking to the safe description.

"I'll leave you in peace, but please have a drink and come out from behind the bar," Demmy requests again.

April nods. "I'll think about it."

"She's a force," says Daniel as Demmy walks away to work the room.

"Yes, she is," April says. "You open wine bottles like a man with experience."

"I have some experience. What can I open for you?"

"Something cold please. This velvet is hot."

"Yes, it is," Daniel says before catching himself. He turns all his effort into opening a bottle of chardonnay. He pours two glasses, toasts with April and says, "You know, looking the way you do in that outfit, it's really a crime to have you hiding behind the bar all night."

April gives an eye roll to Daniel working as an agent for Demmy. Still, a compliment from him and a glass of wine get her out from behind the bar.

After an hour of moving about the room with Daniel facilitating introductions and conversations, the silent auction bid for the elf costume is up to $750. Santa's outfit is only up to $700, so April feels like her efforts are, at the least, not cause for embarrassment. She vows to avoid the bid sheets for the rest of the evening. She's done her part.

As the event winds down, Demmy tells April the elf costume went for $1200—a record. This has April feeling very confident in her elf.

Daniel and April offer to help Demmy clean up, but she insists they leave it to her and the historical committee members. "You've done enough," she says as she hugs April. "Thank you. Mrs. Jensen was thrilled."

"Well," says April, with the tiniest hint of her second glass of wine showing in her delivery, "as long as Mrs. Jensen is happy."

Demmy hugs Daniel too and thanks him for staying for the entire night. "Thank you for helping. That's a long break from your work," she points out very . . . pointedly, as she casts a glance at April.

Daniel ignores the implication. "Anytime," he says.

He and April shuffle into the elevator line. It's a small, slow elevator and if they were less than twelve stories up, the stairs would be a better option.

April gets her phone out to check her messages for the first time in hours. Her mom has called twice. Her dad once. And Lilly has texted several times, asking April to call her back.

April must sigh, because Daniel asks, "Everything okay?"

"Yes, my family is just checking on me." She stops herself. How does she say this? "Uh, my ex is getting married. He called me that day at the store." She tries to lower her voice so no one else in line can hear. She also attempts to say it like it doesn't bother her.

Her plan is to stop there, but she's so uncomfortable with those words just hanging out in the air in front of her that she adds, "For some god awful reason, he told my sister first and she told him he had to tell me, so he did. And now, of course, my sister told my parents. So . . ."

Silence. Oh god, there's the silence. Why did she add the "so" to the end of that sentence?! Now Daniel is waiting for something to follow. "Anyway," she adds, "thanks for the candle."

"Yes," says Daniel as he tries to catch up. "Shit. I'm sorry." He extends his hand to indicate the messages on her phone and also all the words that just spilled out of her mouth. "That's really fucking fast. I'm sorry."

April shrugs.

"And I'm sorry for the other night. I wish I'd just canceled my . . . plans." He doesn't say *date*. "And stayed with you."

"It's okay." April doesn't know what else to say.

"No," says Daniel, "I mean it. I'm sorry about all of it. You deserve better. You deserve . . ." Daniel's words trail off as his gaze falls to the hem of April's costume. As though he's compelled to know how that faux fur lining feels in his hand, he reaches out and rubs the end of April's dress between his thumb and forefinger. "You deserve a lot," he finishes.

He snaps out of it, looking up to find April's equally startled expression. Why did he do that? Why did he touch her clothes like that? It wasn't sexual, but it was intimate in a way that surprises them both.

"I'm sorry," Daniel shakes his head.

"No, it's . . ." April begins, but she doesn't really know what it is, so her sentence ends right there.

They are both relieved to have the elevator door open and swallow their exchange. They shuffle onboard, moving to the back right corner as more people pile in to the box.

Someone at the front keeps holding the door open and encouraging party goers to "squeeze in". It's getting difficult to avoid touching other people. There's one final adjustment moving the inhabitants even closer together so the elevator doors can close.

As the old elevator lurches, all the souls in it laugh nervously. Their bodies jostle. April manages only the briefest encounter with Daniel's shoulder before she's steady on her feet again.

But it doesn't seem like the elevator is moving in the right direction. When the doors pop open almost immediately after closing, it's apparent the machine traveled up one floor to fetch some attendees exploring in the building.

The sardine general up front asks everyone to make room. Who put this guy in charge?

April and Daniel shuffle further into the corner. There is no avoiding each other now. The full length of April's right arm presses against Daniel's left. The backs of their hands touch as the elevator doors close again.

Does Daniel know what he's doing? He seems to move his pinky up and down April's. Before she can confirm that, they stop back on the floor of the party. The doors open to reveal none other than Mrs. Jensen and her cane.

The asshole at the front shouts, "The more the merrier!" And he pushes even further into the elevator.

A very tall man in front of April inches backward. He's about to have his back in full contact with April's chest when Daniel puts a gentle hand on the man's shoulder.

"One second there," he says to the guy as Daniel pulls April into the narrow space in front of him.

"I'm sorry," the man says. He settles into the spot where April just stood. "I didn't see you back there."

Daniel replies to the man. April doesn't hear what he says. She feels it—his breath on her ear as he speaks. Then she's waiting, just waiting for the elevator to move with a jolt. She's bracing herself, but there's no way she's not headed further into Daniel's body.

The door can't close. This is a total shit show and a dangerous one at that. Old elevator. Lots of people. It's a recipe for disaster, and April should not be enjoying it as much as she is. In fact, she silently thanks the drunk guy at the front who keeps packing them in.

Someone makes a joke. April is somewhat aware of people laughing, but she isn't in the crowded elevator anymore. She's only in the corner with Daniel pressed against her backside. Everyone else might as well be a mile away.

The doors manage to close. The elevator jolts (as hoped) as it begins its final descent. Well, hopefully not the final, final descent. April doesn't want to be on an elevator as it stops working, but it's hard to worry about much with Daniel's breath on her neck.

This bounce sends April backward, fully landing against Daniel. His hands grab her hips to steady her. She's so tightly packed between other standing humans, it's not like April could fall. But, you know, she doesn't want to touch other people around her, because that's just rude. So, she has to lean into Daniel instead. His heart beats on her left shoulder blade.

His mouth is near her ear again. His breath tickles her neck. She tries to evenly release the air in her lungs, but it's shaking as it sputters out. Daniel's hands apply gentle pressure on her hips as he takes a deep breath. His lungs fill against the curve of her back. She follows his lead and relaxes into him even further as they breathe out together.

The elevator dings. The doors open. The tall guy shouts from the back, "This is my floor!"

Daniel's hands move to grip the handrails on either side of him. A few people step off to make room for the guy in the back to maneuver forward. When he exits, there's no need for April to fit against Daniel anymore. She stands up straight, putting a few inches between them.

Everyone piles back in. The doors shut. In anticipation of the bump to follow, Daniel and April hold their breath. The elevator lurches downward, and April's left leg has to step back to balance her. Her full leg, from ass to heel, pushes up against Daniel's. His hands tighten their grip on the rails and it makes April smile to notice the way he's white knuckling the brass bar to keep himself from grabbing her instead.

This ride to the first floor seems to last an eternity and, somehow, not nearly long enough. April bites her lip to keep from giggling out of disbelief, or elation—she's not sure which. Daniel's body shakes against her as he also attempts to stifle his laughter.

The elevator lands on the first floor, followed by a mass exodus. Daniel and April shift further out of each other's reach. Daniel holds his arm out to keep the elevator door from shutting. As April passes him, he puts his hand on the small of her back. His palm is warm. It sends warmth out to all the nerves in April's body.

His hand lingers there, on April's lower back, even after she passes the elevator doors. Even after he steps clear of them, too. When his fingers finally leave her, they trail down her spine as they go.

Yes, he does. He knows exactly what he's doing.

The walk from the fundraiser back to the store is awkward for April and Daniel, not because of what just happened on the elevator, but because a tipsy Anna Gale walks with them. Anna doesn't seem to notice that Daniel and April are so charged, they practically have smoke coming off them.

Finally, at the door of Antic Witties (after several false endings), Anna says a goodbye she seems to mean. Just before she walks away, she looks at April as though seeing her for the first time tonight. "You look like an elf," she says. Then she turns on unsteady feet and staggers down the sidewalk.

Daniel and April watch her walk for a moment, not sure she won't turn around and have another story about an antique her husband bought her. When she disappears down the block, they face each other.

Daniel stands in front of the door to the store. "I can't believe I'm about

163

to say this," he begins, "but I really do have work to get done tonight. Joel needs some financial stuff sent by the morning."

"Okay," April nods, but she doesn't move.

"I mean, I wish I didn't. I'd love . . . but I'm already late because of the party tonight."

April keeps nodding. Still doesn't move.

"I'm sorry," Daniel says. "I really do wish I didn't have to get this done."

April finally ends this awkward exchange. "Daniel, I need to come inside to change. My non-elf clothes are in the bathroom."

Now it's Daniel's turn to nod. "Right."

He turns to unlock the door, happy to have an excuse to turn away from April. She heads straight to the bathroom. He heads straight to the front desk.

April changes, leaving the elf costume hanging on the bathroom door. She makes a wide berth around Daniel as he works at the register. She doesn't address him until she's on the other side of the counter.

"I left the costume in the bathroom for tonight, if that's okay."

He looks up from his work. "Of course."

April turns to leave the biggest letdown of letdowns in the history of letting down. And she thought being asked to work after dirty dancing was disappointing . . . that was nothing compared to this brush off.

"April," Daniel says. She turns back, but only when she's safely near the door. Daniel searches for what he wants to say. "You really are a good friend. I mean, what you did for Demmy tonight? You're a good friend, and a . . . great elf."

A good friend. He said that twice.

April nods. "Goodnight, Daniel."

Daniel nods. "Goodnight, April."

28

Charged

After I'd dated this one guy for a couple months, he broke up with me on the way to his friend's wedding. Like, a wedding that was two hours away. Just as we were pulling up to the venue, he told me he didn't want to date me. Then, we sat through a wedding ceremony and a reception where he kept introducing me to everyone as his friend.

I feigned having the best time. I was friendly and outgoing—determined to make his friends like me. They did. He told me on the way home that his friends loved me. I asked if any of them were single. He didn't laugh.

We sat in silence for the other hour and forty-five-minute ride.

It hurt so much. It was the first time someone broke up with me and it really hurt. Now, I'd had crushes that made my bones ache, but this was a new kind of pain—it took over my guts.

I didn't sleep at all that night. The next morning, my dad called to tell me he'd received a tax form for me in the mail. I was already on my way to the house of the guy who'd broken up with me. I left the phone charger for my flip phone plugged into an outlet in his kitchen. I was heading to his house to get my charger back.

Overnight, I convinced myself I needed that charger more than anything in the world. I convinced myself it was totally logical for me to drive across L.A. to the house of the guy who didn't want to see me anymore, because I had to get my flip phone charger.

I convinced myself it made lots of sense to wear the jeans this guy once complimented, and to put on makeup and fix my hair, and look my best to go pick up my phone charger from the guy who broke up with me on the way to his friend's out-of-town wedding.

I'm not sure what prompted me to tell my dad. I guess when your guts are rearranged, you're more prone to being impulsive. I told Dad about the breakup. I told him about the phone charger. I told him I was, at that very minute, on my way to get it. Then I waited for my dad's response.

I wanted him to tell me it was my phone charger and I had every right to go get it. And also, screw that guy for breaking up with me on the way to a wedding. And also, screw that guy for breaking up with me at all.

But that's not what my dad told me.

Instead, he said, "Well, when I played baseball in high school, I aspired to be the catcher, but I lost the position to Billy Turner. I was devastated. He was in my grade, so I figured I'd never be out from underneath him unless I got better than him. I worked my ass off to beat him. I came to workouts before Billy. I put in more time after school than Billy. I ate better than Billy. I tried harder than Billy.

"Finally, my senior year, I go to the coach and complain. I say, 'I've done more than Billy has for years, and I still don't get to be catcher and it's not fair.'

"And the coach says, 'Son, do you know what you and Billy Turner have in common? You both spend all of your time and energy thinking about Billy Turner.'"

That was it. That was how my dad responded to my heartache. Right after telling me that story, he told me he was going to send me the tax form he was calling about, so I should look for it in the mail.

Obviously, that was the first and last time I ever told my dad when my heart was breaking. But I sure exited the freeway right then. And I took my jeans-wearing ass home that day.

Yes, I was heartbroken. But my dad reminded me; I am built for more than trying to catch up to someone who is running away from me. Fuck the phone chargers and all the other desperate excuses our pain creates to keep us focused on the runner who is only focused on the race.

For the rest of my single life, I never tried to get anything back from a guy who didn't want me . . . except my pride.

Excerpt from *Great Expectations* by April Townsend

166

The high from the elevator is way over. Between Anna running drunk interference, Daniel's need to work, and another text from Lilly that reads, *Call me,* April's sexual vibe is no longer vibing. In fact, it's turned to dread.

Call me texts are never good news. April gets it over with. She calls her sister on the way home from the elf party.

The phone only rings once before Lilly picks up with a "Hi."

It's not a good "hi". It's a very bad "hi". It's an, "I need to acknowledge I answered your call while simultaneously warning you I'm gonna talk about something really shitty" kind of "hi".

"What is it?" April braces herself for the answer.

"She's pregnant," Lilly says.

"Morgan's girlfriend?" April asks, even though the answer is obvious.

"Yes," says Lilly.

Shit.

Shit. Shit. Shit.

Shitty shit.

Here's that god awful feeling again—guts flipping inside out. She's not surprised by this news. She had the awful thought this might be the case. She had the weird, baby-Evan dream. But having the bad thought and the weird dream still didn't prepare her for the reveal.

How many times can one person break her heart? Every time. Every fucking time she thinks she's crawling out from under Morgan's reach, she ends up back underneath him. "So, did he call you or what?"

"I saw it online," Lilly says.

"He posted it online?!" That's . . . that's a special punch in the balls. "So everyone knows before me?"

"Would you have preferred he called and told you?" Lilly isn't being glib. She honestly wonders how it would be best to find out the man you were married to through all of your child-bearing years is now having a baby with someone he just met.

"I don't know." April isn't crying. She won't let herself, or she's too damn tired of feeling this way to make the effort. "Listen, thank you for telling me, but I gotta go, okay?"

Lilly isn't so sure. "Okay, but can I come see you? I could come right after I drop the kids off in the morning."

"No. No. I'm okay," says April.

She's not okay.

"I've got a plan," she says.

She doesn't have a plan.

"Really?" Lilly sounds hopeful.

"Yes. Definitely."

No. Nope. She's got nothing.

April hangs up after telling her sister she loves her. She doesn't have a plan, but she's sure as hell not going home and being alone with her phone.

She pulls over and texts Demmy to ask if she's still cleaning up the party. There's no reply. She can't bother Mimi with her wedding so close. She sure as shit will not bother Buzz-Kill Danny while he's working.

Screw it. It's a terrible idea, but she's suddenly having a terrible night. It's 11:30, that means there's time for one drink before the bar at Buckneye's closes.

So this is what it's like to go to a bar alone. It's both more and less scary than doing so in L.A. In L.A., April would likely walk into a room full of strangers. In Cleo, April is likely walking into a room with at least one person she knows.

It's hard to say which situation is less safe.

April scans the bar and doesn't see anyone she recognizes. She notes a tiny ping of disappointment.

"He's not here," a voice behind her says.

April spins around to see Alice.

"I'm not looking for Evan," April says. Alice's eyes don't actually move, but she rolls her eyes in intention, and April feels every bit of it. It's an admirable trick.

"Alright," April gives in, "the thought may have occurred to me, but only because I'm desperate for a distraction."

"You've come to the right place," says Alice. April can hear now the slight slur in her usually precise enunciation. Alice leads April to the bar, where a napkin over a seat suggests Alice was using it as a seat saver. Before ordering "two specials" from the bartender, Alice removes the napkin and gestures for April to sit on the barstool next to her.

"What's the special?" April asks.

Alice shrugs. "It's green and it works." April accepts this. "So how was the elf costume?" Alice asks.

"It was green and it worked," says April.

Alice gives her the side eye. She seems to hate herself for asking, but she does it anyway. "And how was Santa?"

"Fine, I think. I honestly didn't talk to him except for a photo op. He was very busy."

"Always is," says Alice.

The bartender delivers the specials. The ladies cheers and sip. It's an apple martini. Probably.

"Are you waiting for Evan?" April asks.

Alice looks deep into her drink. "Of course not. I just came to have one drink to relax after work. And then, he wasn't here when I finished that one, so I needed another one while I answered some emails on my phone. And then he still wasn't here, so now I'm here having a third drink so I can talk to you."

"I'm sorry," April says.

Alice lets out all the air in her lungs. "I'm not mad at him, of course. I'm never mad at him. He's been nothing other than what he says he is. But here I am. Again."

April wonders for a moment if she should spill the truth to Alice. In some way, it seems like Alice is her enemy or supposed to be her enemy, but all she sees tonight is a beautiful, tipsy, self-loathing soul.

"If it makes you feel any better, my ex-husband is getting married and having a baby."

Alice looks at April. "Thank you. That does make me feel better."

"Good," says April, "glad I can be of some use."

Alice holds her glass up to toast. "Well, here's to the happy couple. May they have a healthy baby that never sleeps through the night."

April lifts her glass to cheers.

"So you're still in love with him or what?" Alice asks.

"Good question," April begins. "I don't understand how I can hurt this much if I don't love him."

"Oh," Alice makes a face, "No, you can't trust that hurt. That hurt is not honest. It makes you do crazy shit, right? I mean, people say love makes you do crazy shit, but really it's the hurt."

April is beginning to like tipsy Alice.

Alice continues, "Like, I don't think I'm in love with Evan. I don't obsess over him and do stupid shit, illogical shit, to be near him because I'm in love with him. I'm . . . in pain with him. You know?" Alice looks to April for affirmation. "And the pain makes me, like, not trust myself. Like, I can't trust myself, because my body betrays me when he's near me and it's not even sexual, I mean . . . it is . . ." Alice raises her eyebrows as she looks pointedly at April. "But it's all this confusing shit in the middle, too." She indicates her midsection. "And I want to set it all in order. I want to stop hurting. And the quickest way to do that is to be with him. So I come sit at the bar he frequents and I wait. And he shows up or he doesn't show up; I wake up and do it all over again tomorrow. And every time I wait for him, I trust myself a little less." Alice nods in agreement with her own words. "Or maybe I'm just drunk."

"Well," April offers, "at least you didn't dress like an elf tonight."

"Hey," Alice blinks slowly, "two steps forward, two steps back."

April drives Alice home. As Alice gets out of the car, April says, "You know, you made it an entire night without him. That's a good first step."

Alice doesn't look convinced. "I mean, I got trashed by myself at a bar instead."

"Yes," April smiles. "By yourself."

Alice's expression is hard to read. "Thanks for the ride," she calls over her shoulder as she turns to head up the sidewalk. After a few steps, she stops, throws her head back with a sigh of frustration, then turns back to April. "Fuck the phone chargers, right?"

It takes April a moment to realize what Alice is asking. She's surprised to find out Alice read *Great Expectations.* Maybe this is an invitation for new friendship or . . . ah, yes. She understands now.

"Right," April says. "There's no good reason to go over to his house tonight."

"But, see…" Alice scrunches up her face, "I've got all these excellent justifications."

"Fuck 'em," says April. "You can't trust the hurt, right?"

"Right," says Alice. "That's right." And she turns to walk up her driveway and disappear into her house.

29

Book Burning

The next morning, April blocks Morgan's number on her phone. She blocks him on her social media accounts (even though she quit using them the day they separated). She deletes his number (though she obviously has it memorized). She deletes every email he ever sent her. She texts Lilly and asks her to block Morgan too, and to unfollow his baby-announcing ass on social media.

She borrows the fire pit in Demmy's backyard, and burns every item she has remaining with Morgan's name or picture on it—including boxes of old tax paperwork and their marriage certificate.

It's all largely symbolic, of course. You can't set your heartache on fire and watch it go up in smoke, but you can sure try.

For the finale, April pulls out her very first printed edition of *Great Expectations,* which she removed from its hiding place this morning. It's like she's holding her failure in a neat little six-by-nine inch, two-hundred-and-fifty-one page rectangle. The book weighs less than a pound, but it feels like it weighs more than April.

As April lifts it over the smoke of the fire, Demmy comes running out of the house.

"Wait!" she yells. "Just wait," she says quietly once April has pulled the book back from the fire. Demmy stares at her friend through the black smoke. They face each other with the fire pit in between them.

"What is that?" Demmy asks about the book in April's hand.

"I think you know what it is."

"Is it just a copy from any ol' bookstore in the world, or is it something of value?"

"It's not of value anymore," says April. "That's the problem."

"You know what? I asked the wrong person," says Demmy. "I ask you what's in your hand and you don't know. You have no idea what that book is to anyone who has read it. That's the problem. You think that story belongs to you. You don't give your readers any credit."

Those words sting. "The readers are who I'm worried about," says April. "I failed people who believed in the shit I wrote about in here. It's embarrassing."

"That's what I'm talking about right there," says Demmy. "YOU are embarrassed. Don't put that shit on your fans.

"You think your book is about you and Morgan, but your book is about the person reading it. What do they think about the dude washing the dishes at a strip club? When did they ever have a guy look past them to see if something better was in the room? People don't love your book because of what it means to you, they love it because of what it means to them. And you don't control that.

"If you think your readers are disappointed in you for getting divorced, then you underestimate us AND you don't even understand your own words.

"And I'm sorry if I'm being harsh. I'm just freaked out because I don't want you to burn something you can't get back." Demmy looks at the book April holds near the fire.

April pulls *Great Expectations* further from danger.

Demmy softens. "And for what it's worth, all my favorite parts of the book have absolutely nothing to do with Morgan. The red leather jacket? I think about it every time I go thrift shopping."

April looks skeptical. "When do you ever go thrift shopping?"

"Once," Demmy confesses. "I went once. But I thought of that chapter. And I think of your book every single time a client puts his hand on my back to usher me through a door at a listing. Before I read about that, it didn't even occur to me to have an opinion on the subject. And every time I pass dishes for sale anywhere, I picture the nearest guy humping the bowls. It makes me very happy."

"Really," April says casually, "my greatest contribution to society is giving people that visual." She looks at the book in her hand. "I don't know. I feel like this is the thing still tying me to Morgan. Like, he's moved on. And I'm still stuck inside this cover."

"Stuck?!" says Demmy. "Are you still living in L.A.?" It's a rhetorical question and April doesn't plan to answer, but Demmy doesn't plan to stop waiting for April to answer.

After ten uncomfortable seconds of a staring contest, April replies, "No."

"Did you move yourself halfway across the country and buy your own damn house?"

"Yes."

"Did you start not just one, but two new jobs recently?"

"Do you really expect me to answer each question?"

"Yes," Demmy answers.

"Then, yes," April answers.

"You hosted a big fundraising event, raised something like over a hundred thousand for the children, is that something you've done before?"

"No."

"Did you have prior experience running into a statue's balls before you ran into Coach Basham a few weeks ago?"

"I did not."

"You dressed like an elf last night. Is that something your into on the regular?"

"No, actually, I just have this horrible friend . . ."

"If you wanted to drive naked through the Burger Barn drive-thru right now, and order ten milkshakes and a small fry, would anyone stop you from doing that?"

"Besides the police?" April asks.

"Besides the police," Demmy answers.

"No, no one would stop me."

"Because you are unstoppable, April. You are the least stuck person I know. You've got to give yourself more credit."

30

In Tiers

When I was twelve, my family was having a garage sale. This mom, dad, and young daughter show up toward the end. It's clear they don't have a lot of money. They're looking around; they ask if I'm selling any toys. I tell them I sold all the toys. So they start to leave, but I tell them to wait. I run into my room and, for some reason, I grab my Christmas Barbie.

Now Christmas Barbie was one of my prized possessions when I got her on my tenth Christmas. She has a beautiful red dress that's velvet on top, then flows down in puffy layers of tulle and glitter. I was always afraid to play with her because I didn't want to mess her up. But now, I sell her to this little girl for 50 cents.

As soon as this family leaves, I regret selling my Christmas Barbie. I'd begged my parents to buy her for me. I'd been so thrilled to get her. Now, I just couldn't stop being sad I'd given her away.

I tell my mom what's bothering me. I tell her I wasn't quite ready to give up that doll. I don't know what possessed me to give it to someone else. I'm afraid I made a mistake.

Mom tells me that knowing when to give something up is one of the hardest things to learn in life. "Because most of the time," she says, "the only way to know if you've held on too long or given up too fast, is to do it."

Seeing that this depressing life lesson did not, in any way, cheer me up, Mom asks me what the little girl did when I gave her the doll.

"She hugged it," I say.

Mom puts her arm around me and pulls me close. She asks me when I last hugged that Barbie.

I say, "I can't remember."

She says, "I don't think it's a mistake to give something you like to someone who can love it."

Excerpt from *Great Expectations* by April Townsend

The day after attempting to burn Morgan out of her life, April gives her two weeks' notice to Daniel. Two weeks will get them to the new year. Daniel won't need both April and Mimi once the holidays are over. April decides to spare all three of them the awkward situation.

By delivering the news in front of Mimi, April also spares Daniel the opportunity to ask if her leaving has anything to do with the letdown of the elevator-foreplay-followed-by-work incident. Which it doesn't. Mostly.

Daniel seems to take the resignation in stride. He might even seem to be a little relieved.

The next week goes by in a blur. Three hundred and fifty-two presents wrapped. Even Mimi, with all her youthful energy, is too exhausted to interact much. Daniel and April don't talk about anything but work. There's no opportunity for bourbon in the break room.

April doesn't decorate her house for Christmas. Somehow it seems more sad to attempt making her sad house seem festive, than to just leave it looking, you know . . . sad.

She buys gifts for her nieces and nephew online and gets some small things for her parents and Lilly from Antic Witties. She wraps the hell out of those gifts—especially Lilly's.

April agrees to drive to Houston on Christmas Eve, only if she can leave after lunch on Christmas Day with no grumbling from her family.

It's not that she doesn't love her family. It's that she can only take twenty-four hours of the concerned looks and the worried whispers behind her back. It's the pity that has her dreading the holiday with her kin.

As she prepares to leave Antic Witties on December twenty-third, April debates whether to run out the door or to give Daniel the small Christmas gift she has for him in her purse. It's just a set of watercolors she spotted at the craft store when she and Mimi were shopping for wedding decorations. They're in a metal tin that says, *Paint or Dye Trying.*

She already gave Mimi two pens; one engraved with her maiden name and one with her soon-to-be-married name. The card read, *So you can write your future and your history.*

Mimi loved them. She gave April homemade Christmas cookies decorated like little elves, which Mimi thought was hilarious.

April decides she's too self-conscious to give the watercolors to Daniel. She ditches the idea and heads for the door as she calls, "Happy holidays!" to Daniel over her shoulder.

Daniel looks up in alarm. "Wait! I've got something for you." He reaches under the counter to pull out an envelope and a wrapped package. "Merry Christmas."

Mimi comes squealing out of the wrapping room. "Wait for me! I want to watch her open it."

April approaches the gifts laid out for her and kicks herself for not giving Daniel the watercolors. Now if she gives the gift, it will seem like she's only giving it because he gave her one. She sets her purse down on the counter and opens the envelope first.

"Oh, that's just money," Mimi interrupts.

Daniel gives Mimi a look. "If money isn't important to you, please feel free to give your bonus back."

Mimi ignores him. "Open the present," she says to April.

It's obvious Mimi wrapped the package, so April tries to be respectful of her efforts by carefully unwrapping it. But Mimi doesn't have the patience.

"Oh, just tear it!" she demands.

April tears off one strip of paper and recognizes what lies beneath. She looks at Daniel with wide eyes.

"I tried to get you a real one," he says, "but the only one I could find sold in 2018."

"I told him to draw it," Mimi says proudly. "I said it was better this way, anyway." Mimi rips off the rest of the wrapping job because April is too damn slow.

It's a framed sketch of April's Christmas Barbie. Barbie's hair and body are in the graphite color of a pencil. Her head is turned, looking over her shoulder. Her arms are posed like she's dancing with an imaginary Ken. The red tiered dress is the only thing in color. It looks like it's moving—as though Barbie is mid-spin.

April doesn't say anything.

"It's the right one, isn't it?" Mimi asks. "We only found one picture online with the red tulle layers on the dress."

"It's the right one," April says.

"Mimi framed it." Daniel tries to read April's expression. "It's not a big deal," he adds.

Mimi is insulted. "I spent two hours matting that!"

"I mean the sketch. The whole idea. It's not a big . . ."

April cuts Daniel off by hugging the drawing to her chest and wrapping her arms around it.

"I love it," she says.

And she does.

31

Biggie Smalls

The twenty-four-hour-holiday-with-family-a-thon is not so bad. It's clear the adults in April's family have an agreement to avoid bringing up Morgan, marriage, and babies.

During Christmas Eve dinner, April's mom tells Lilly that a neighbor just had a baby. Mrs. Townsend catches her mistake, glances at April in horror, and cuts herself off mid-sentence. Then she asks if anyone needs more mashed potatoes.

April is too sentimental to be annoyed. She can see her parents have slowed down. Her mom takes longer to pass out presents. Her dad takes longer to make coffee.

April vows to come here more often. In fact, she can't quite remember what she was so busy doing the past few holiday seasons she couldn't make it to her family.

Her nieces and nephew are different people than the last time she saw them in person. Even though she's seen lots of photos of them growing up, it's jarring to see them in three dimensions.

As April watches them open presents on Christmas morning, she tries to be honest with herself. Does she wish she had kids of her own?

She and Morgan never wanted kids. But did SHE want kids? Was not having children another whole-milk-compromise she made in exchange for having Morgan?

She can't say for certain, and she takes that as a positive sign. Probably, if she isn't sure she wants kids, she shouldn't have them. And she isn't. So she shouldn't. Let Morgan, in his late-forties, stay up all night with a newborn. April will get some sleep.

"So how's Cleo?" her dad asks as they sit on the back porch wrapped in the blankets Lilly gave them for Christmas. It's just April and her father for the moment. Lilly and her mother make french toast inside.

"It's good I think," says April.

"I never thought you liked it there much."

"Yeah, well, it's small. When I was a teenager, I felt like I was too big for a small town."

"And now?"

"Now I feel small. So it fits." April is as surprised by those words as her father looks.

"April." Her father says her name in a way that makes April fifteen-years-old-again. She meets his stare, daring him to argue with her.

He doesn't. He turns his attention back to the yard he keeps well manicured.

"You know," he says finally, "when your mom and I were going to move here, we decided we were finally going to live in our dream house we'd been talking about for decades. We wanted a pool and four bedrooms for when you girls and your families visited. Wanted at least an acre of land, a dining room, three full bathrooms, and a wrap-around porch. We looked at so many houses, I thought our real estate agent was going to fire us."

April looks at the pool-less backyard and the small porch she sits on. It's beautiful here, but it's not any of the things her father just named.

"So one day, we're looking at a house a couple miles down from here. We happen to pass this place and there's a for sale sign out front. Your mom asks me about it later that night. She says, 'What if we looked at the cute little house we passed today?'

"I said, 'But that's not the house we've always dreamed of living in.'

"And she said, 'Maybe we need to be looking at a house we want to die in.'"

"Dad!" April protests, but he holds up his hand to silence her.

"It's not a bad thing, April, to realize what you used to want isn't what you want anymore. I don't want to mow an acre anymore. Your mom doesn't want to clean three bathrooms. Neither of us wants to keep up a pool.

"It turns out, we don't want to spend our remaining years taking care of a big house. We want to take care of each other. It is a strange thing to wake up and discover that what you used to think of as 'settling for less' might actually be the best thing you can do for yourself.

"Maybe you find yourself in a small town. But, April," Coach Townsend twists in his chair to fully face his youngest daughter, "YOU are not small. You never have been. You never will be."

When April arrives back in Cleo, she drives through downtown. It's dusk. The giant Christmas tree is lit in the middle of the street. People gather around it snapping photos. Christmas lights outline the tops of all the buildings.

April pulls over a little distance from the crowd. She gets out of her car to the muggy warmth of a Texas Christmas. *Once Upon a Christmas*, the album by Kenny Rogers and Dolly Parton, plays out of the open window of a loft nearby.

By tomorrow it might be freezing. The weather here is impossible to predict. But tonight it feels comfortable.

32

That's a Wrap

The day after Christmas is one of the Antic Witties busiest days of the year. They don't have many returns, but they have a ton of shoppers for their New Year's Sale. Plus all holiday items are half off.

Though they are all exhausted from a busy day, Daniel and April toast Mimi at closing time. It's her last day until after her wedding.

"When I come back through those doors," Mimi says, "I'll be married."

As Mimi and April exit together after the toast, April claims to have forgotten something in the break room. She tells Mimi to go on without her, then she doubles back to find Daniel in the stockroom. She pulls the watercolors, wrapped in brown butcher paper, out of her purse.

"I have a little Christmas gift for you," she says as she extends the package. "I had it before Christmas, but I was too embarrassed to give it to you."

"Why?" Daniel crosses to April to take the present.

"Well," says April, "I guess because I'm embarrassed about a lot of things these days. But I'm trying to not let that stop me from . . ."

From what? Trying? Living? How does she end this thought?

"From giving little gifts, I guess."

"Okay," says Daniel, as though that makes perfect sense.

"I'll see you tomorrow," April says as she turns on her heels and has to keep herself from running to the door.

Five minutes later, her phone pings with a text from Daniel.

Daniel: It's my favorite gift I got this year.

Her phone pings again.

Daniel: Don't tell Mimi I said that.

The next few days at the store are busy wrapping and delivering all of Mimi's registry items. April, of course, purchases a serving bowl for Mimi and Omar. The card reads, *For best results, wash with care.*

On April's last day, she's disappointed to find Joel doing paperwork in the wrapping room. She'd hoped for an after work toast with Daniel. Instead, she gets a sincere thank you and a handshake from both her bosses. After the way April and Daniel touched in the elevator a few weeks ago, a handshake is laughable. They both seem to agree on this because they avoid eye contact to keep from laughing.

Daniel manages a brief moment alone with April as he walks her to the front door. "Thank you again," he says. "It's been nice getting to . . . work with you. I'll see you at the wedding?"

"I'll be there," says April. Daniel opens the door. As April passes through it, she remembers the costume. "Oh, the elf dress is still hanging in the bathroom."

"That's okay," smiles Daniel. "I own it."

He closes and locks the door to Antic Witties without acknowledging April's stunned expression on the other side of the glass.

33

Making Up

Mimi's wedding day is warm for December. April wakes with a sense of dread. She's happy for Mimi, of course, but weddings aren't exactly the sought after event of the recently divorced.

Tomorrow is New Year's Eve. She's not looking forward to that either. Demmy has invited her to a party at the lake, but April's not sure she has the energy to be around a bunch of drunk people on the last day of the worst year of her life.

She takes her time getting ready for the wedding, and finishes by slipping on the blue silk dress she originally bought for the elf event. The dress is like a mullet, conservative in the front and a party in the back. The back cuts dramatically low—not exactly revealing, but definitely outside April's comfort zone. Of course, that's where she's been living for much of the past year, so she's trying to embrace it.

She digs in her closet for her gold high heels. They aren't stilettos because she's not willing to be in that much pain for any event, but they are the tallest she's got. They make her feel powerful.

The wedding is in an event space downtown, just a couple blocks from Antic Witties. As April approaches the venue, she spots Daniel's truck parked in front of the store. Though sudden decisions to stop for men while driving downtown haven't worked for her in the past, she pulls into a parking spot.

Daniel exits the building with a beautifully wrapped gift box—if April does say so herself. Inside the beautifully wrapped gift box is Daniel's present to the couple; a $150 blanket (and not the used one from the tornado party either—a brand new one).

April watches Daniel place the box on the hood of his truck and return to lock up. He's wearing a button-up shirt with a sports jacket and blue jeans that fit him very well. April doesn't consider herself a cowboy fan, but she may have to rethink that because there's something about Daniel in boots she doesn't mind at all.

By the time he turns around from locking the door, April is leaning on the front of his truck. She looks at Daniel's feet and tries to sound cool and casual as she says, "Nice boots."

Only, "nice boots" are not the words that come out of her mouth. Instead, she sounds cool and casual as she says to Daniel, "Nice boobs."

She says. To Daniel. Nice. Boobs. She squeezes her eyes shut, but not before she sees Daniel's eyebrows lift along with the corners of his mouth.

"Boots," she corrects herself. "Nice boots." Well, there was no need for her to have applied blush on her cheeks.

"They're brand new," he says as he puts the gift in his truck. "I need to break them in on the dance floor."

"Can I help with that?" April asks.

"I hope so," Daniel says. He leans on the hood beside April. They stare at their reflection in the store window.

"How are you doing today?" he asks.

"I'm okay I think."

"You look okay," he says.

"Yeah?"

"Yeah."

"You look okay too," she says.

"Do you like my boobs?" he asks.

April keeps staring straight ahead. Daniel nudges her shoulder with his. He's smiling at her in their reflection. She smiling back.

"Who are those two people there?" she asks as she nods toward their image.

"Those two?" Daniel says as he points to the Daniel and the April in the window staring back at them. "Oh, those are two troublemakers."

"I thought so," says April. "They're friends, obviously."

"They try to be," Daniel says.

"Why do they try?" April asks.

"I think," Daniel is slow to answer, "because they like each other a lot. They respect each other a lot. And they want to be sure no one gets hurt a lot."

"Okay," April tries to be sure she understands, "so he's worried he'll hurt her?"

Daniel shakes his head at their reflection. "You give me too much credit." He turns to April. "I'm covering my own ass."

April holds the present in her lap while Daniel drives them the few blocks to the wedding. As soon as they walk in the front door of the event space, Demmy flutters over.

"Mimi has been looking for you," she says to April.

"For me?!" April asks in surprise. "Is everything okay?"

Demmy shrugs in an unusually panicked way, which makes April's nerves start bristling. Daniel offers to save them a seat as Demmy escorts April upstairs to the bridal room.

"Good luck," says Demmy as she opens the door for April to enter.

April slips into the room to find Mimi surrounded by her mother and two bridesmaids in long red dresses. The bride is backlit by an enormous window overlooking downtown. She looks like an angel.

Mimi's mother glares at April with a glare that says, "Do not fuck up this day I have planned for months."

April puts her hands up as if surrendering. She approaches with caution. "Mimi, you're stunning."

"Thank you," Mimi says.

"I was told you want to see me." April tries to sound like this is commonplace. All brides summon her on their wedding day.

"Yes," Mimi applies a smile that's almost convincing. "This is my mom, Betty." Betty does not offer a hand to April. Mimi seems unfazed as she turns to the ladies in red. "And this is my cousin, Amy, who also did my makeup,

187

and my college roommate, Carissa."

The bridesmaids are much friendlier than the mother of the bride. April shakes hands with them. "Beautiful job on the makeup. Nice to meet you both."

Mimi looks meaningfully at her mother and, after a tense moment, the woman caves. "We'll be right outside," she says as she exits with the two bridesmaids toddling after her.

As soon as the door closes, Mimi whispers to April, "It's too much. I don't even feel like myself." Mimi shakes her hands on the side of her face for emphasis as she speaks.

April attempts to keep her eyes from bulging out in panic.

"It's awful, right?" asks Mimi.

"No. Mimi, no," April tries to stall as she silently prays she'll have the right words. She guides the bride over to a couch to sit. April helps Mimi arrange her dress as she formulates an approach. April is a terrible liar and Mimi knows her well enough to sniff out her bullshit.

April thinks of Daniel, of the way he talked about his marriage with no sense of failure, of the way he talked about the girl who twirled fire as though she was a good memory. April tries for a moment to see her marriage as though it could exist outside the context of the divorce . . . and Morgan's engagement . . . and his baby.

She tries to tell the truth from that perspective.

"Marriage is not awful. I loved it for so many years. It freed me in a lot of ways. It rooted me and gave me room to stretch out. Even knowing how it ends, I would relive my wedding day. I'd relive it all if I got to do it over again, because . . . because I ended up where I'm meant to be, and marriage was a huge part of that process."

Mimi's concerned expression hasn't left her face. "Oh my god," she says slowly, "I'm so glad to hear you say that. Thank you." Mimi throws her arms around April in a hug. Then she pulls back, still looking concerned. She pats April's knee. "But I was talking about my makeup."

"What?"

"I was trying to tell you my makeup is too much, and I'm asking your opinion."

"Oh!" says April. "Shit. Oh shit."

Mimi barely hides a smile. "What did you think THIS meant?" Mimi redoes the gesture with her hands shaking at the side of her face for emphasis. April now understands that gesture for what it is . . . an emphasis on Mimi's face.

April laughs in horror. "I'm so sorry. I thought this was like wedding jitters or something," April says as she mimics the hand shaking.

"You think wedding jitters are literal jitters?" Mimi laughs.

"I don't know!" April squeals. "You called me in here. I freaked out."

"It took Amy two hours to do my makeup. I didn't have the heart to tell her I hate it."

April looks over Mimi's face. Yes, without backlighting, it's easier to see Mimi's makeup—of which there is a lot, and what appears to be three rows of eyelashes. They look like shark teeth.

"Well," says April, "from the back of the church, it's gonna be amazing."

Mimi's wedding starts in twenty minutes. "I don't care what the people in the back of the church see. Omar is not even going to recognize me."

"Oh, Mimi!" April feels desperate. Her friend called in the wrong help. "I'm not good at makeup!"

"I know," says Mimi.

Okay. Ouch.

"I wanted to text you, but Amy was taking pictures with my phone. I need the makeup kit from my cubby at the store and the makeup wipes I keep on the bathroom shelf. And I need some excuse for Amy."

Alright. These are things April can help with. She pulls Mimi to her feet while reaching for a bottle of water on the table. "Is your mascara waterproof?" she asks.

"No. I'm not really a crier," says Mimi.

"You are today," says April. "Bend over."

"Uh, there are other ways to make me cry!" Mimi puts her hands on the snack table and leans forward. It's good to hear her sense of humor is still intact.

April tucks a cloth napkin in Mimi's cleavage to protect the white dress, then she pours water on her own fingers and dabbles drops of it onto Mimi's third row of lashes. It doesn't take much. There's enough mascara to paint an entire black box theatre, and it's now running in streaks down Mimi's face.

April pulls the napkin from the top of the dress and hands it to Mimi to hold under her chin. April pats her friend on the shoulder. "I'll be right back."

As April rushes past Mimi's mom and bridesmaids just outside the door, she blurts, "I'm so sorry. I didn't mean to make her cry. I'll get some wipes."

April is several steps out the front door of the building when she realizes she no longer has keys to the shop. She makes a u-turn and dodges wedding guests as she tries to hurry without looking flustered.

In the main room, many guests are already seated in neat rows; it takes April a moment to spot Daniel. He's sitting in the middle of a row, saving the seat next to him.

April comes to the end of his line of chairs. The people closest to her stand as soon as she arrives, but she says, "Oh no. No. No. I actually just need him to come out." She smiles too much as she points to Daniel and motions for him to come toward her. He also masks his concern with a forced smile as he shuffles past the other guests in the row.

April takes his arm and pulls him all the way out of the building. "I need to get in the shop to get some things for Mimi."

"Is she okay?" Daniel asks as he pulls his keys out. "I could drive around to the alley and she could escape out the back door." He planned this out while he waited.

"Good to know, but I think she just needs some makeup."

Daniel's adrenaline is pumping. Even if he doesn't have to pull off an escape, he's ready for a quest. He treats the drive to the store like it's a live or die situation. He runs two yellow lights and pulls up, parallel to Antic Witties, with a squeal of his tires. He takes up three parking spots like a rebel, jumps out of his truck, and has the door to the shop open in record time.

April is not in such a hurry that she doesn't notice the hormone rush she's getting from this version of Daniel—who asks no questions and takes no particular parking spots.

April finds the requested makeup items in the bathroom. As she exits the shop, it's like she and Daniel are in a slow-motion movie moment. They move in sync, as though choreographed. Daniel opens the shop door just as April approaches. He puts his hand on the small of her back as she steps over the threshold. She looks over her right shoulder to see him locking up and, by the time she looks forward again, he's come around her left side and opened his driver's side door for April to crawl through to her side. They share a smile.

She steps up into his truck, tossing Mimi's items to the passenger seat. Then she hikes her dress up with both hands and crawls onto the seat behind the steering wheel so she can scoot to her side. Daniel is close behind her.

Really close.

Too close.

He steps up into his truck, and face plants into her ass. It hurts her tailbone, so she knows it hurts his face.

"Oh!" he yelps, as he leans into the horn while grasping for his nose. The movie moment has come to a screeching halt. April imagines the record scratch in her head. She crawls to her side of the truck as both sets of her cheeks burn.

"Sorry," she can hear Daniel say, followed by a giggle. It takes a moment for her to realize the giggle belongs to her.

"What is it about you and my ass, Danny?" she says as she stares straight ahead.

"I just love it," he answers. Then he flips a u-turn back to the wedding.

They are the unsung heroes of the day. At the reception, Daniel and April toast each other for their bravery in the face of adversity. They watch Mimi and Omar enjoy their first dance. The bride is sporting one-third of the makeup she had on an hour ago.

She looks gorgeous. They look so in love.

April has a little pinch in her heart, but it's not so bad. Maybe she really meant what she said to Mimi in the bridal room. It's possible, somewhere in the very-distant-future, she'll be able to see her marriage as a good chapter in her life.

Feeling Daniel's hand splayed on the small of her back, having his warmth radiate through her silk dress, knowing that in a few minutes, he'll ask her to dance . . . makes anything seem possible.

34

It's All Sober

Morgan would dance when April asked him to. He was what people would call a "good sport" about it. But he didn't get the same joy from dancing that April did. Just like she didn't get the same joy from playing golf that he did. It was fine. She didn't need a partner who shared all her hobbies.

But, damn.

Dancing with Daniel is so much fun. Not only is he an excellent two-step partner, but he dances in all the styles to all the songs. Now, he is not going to win any competitions in free-style, but he doesn't care. He's moving any way that feels right to him. He's free.

It's glorious.

April can't determine if she's tipsy from the mojitos or the moves, but she doesn't give it too much thought because she's . . . tipsy. She's just euphoric enough to get lost in the moment.

When the DJ announces he's playing the last song, April is desperate to keep the high. Daniel's hands on her hips feel like they are vibrating. The backs of her arms buzz where they touch his chest and shoulders as her hands wrap around his neck. Her head swims in some alternate reality where dancing dissolves all complications.

It would be so easy to kiss him. She would only have to lean forward and tilt her chin up a few . . .

No. Nope. She's not drunk. She's still got a line, and other people in town seeing her kiss Daniel is across that line.

Just like that, the buzz is gone and the future is here. April stops swaying to the music.

"You okay?" Daniel asks the question, but he already knows the answer. Back to reality.

"We should go," says April. "I don't want to overstay our welcome." They are one of only three couples left on the dance floor. Mimi and Omar left thirty minutes ago. Demmy has been gone for hours.

Daniel drops April off at her car. He offers to drive her home as he pulls into a parking spot facing his store window.

"No," she says. "I'm sober. Unfortunately."

"Unfortunately?" His eyebrows raise.

"There's part of me wishing I was too tipsy to drive, so you'd have to take me home."

"Mmm," he nods. "There's part of me wishing I was drunk enough to not be the me who didn't drink much so that I could be sober enough to take you home if you needed a ride."

April can see their reflection in the store window again. "Those poor bastards. Too responsible to fuck up their friendship."

"What sad, little, lonely assholes," Daniel replies.

For old time's sake, April listens to "Possession" by Sarah McLachlan on repeat all the way home. She pulls into her driveway, looking up to the bedroom window where she once put all her romantic hopes and dreams.

She turns the car off with a sigh and opens the door.

"Hey," says a familiar voice as she climbs out of her car. April turns to see Daniel walking toward her from where he parked his truck in front of her house.

"Hey," she says in surprise as she shuts her door.

"I was thinking," he says, "maybe it's a good thing we're sober. Because now, if we do something stupid, we both know the other person is doing the stupid thing out of sheer stupidity and not out of vodka."

April smiles. She smiles so big it feels like her face can't contain it. "Are we about to fuck up our friendship?" she asks.

"I don't know," says Daniel. "I hope so."

April leans against her driver's side as Daniel steps closer. His arms lift to either side of her head. His palms push against her car as he leans into her. They're still smiling like two idiots.

Their first kiss is all teeth and giggles. But the second one is not. They both take it very seriously. Now, they are drunk on each other.

Daniel pushes off the car and runs his right hand down April's arm until he's holding her hand. "Can I come in, please?" he asks.

"Yes," April says. "Yes, you can."

35

Catching Air

Sex on an air mattress isn't ideal when you're a twenty-something living in the first apartment you pay for by yourself.

Sex on an air mattress when you're a forty-something living in your first house since getting a divorce is also, as it turns out, not ideal.

At one point, in the act of shifting positions, Daniel lands too hard on the left side of the air mattress and April bounces right off the right side of the bed.

This occurs after April trips up the stairs while trying to kick off her gold heels, and after the cuffs of Daniel's button-down shirt absolutely refuse to slide over his hands. They still don't have that shirt off his wrists when April bounces to the floor.

She's now lying on her back next to the air mattress, staring up at the ceiling. Her mullet dress is still intact, but her pride is exposed. The last time she got bounced like that was off her trampoline in third grade, and she still hasn't entirely recovered from that fright.

"Are you still there?" asks Daniel from on top of the air mattress.

"No," April answers flatly.

"Oh good," he replies, "because if you were still there on the floor, I couldn't help you. My arms are stuck."

April sits up and looks over to see Daniel lying in his tank top with his hands pinned to his sides. His shirt cuffs are like a pair of handcuffs around his wrists, with the rest of his button-down (having been pulled off his shoulders, down his back and the length of his arms as far as it would go before being cock-blocked by his cuffs) lying underneath the weight of his body—making it impossible for him to move his arms.

He looks funny. She feels ridiculous.

"I'll rescue you, " says April.

She gathers all her strength in order to crawl on the floor to the other side of the bed. She kneels next to Daniel.

"Can you sit up?" she asks.

Though Daniel's abs suggest he's very capable of a sit up, the shifting weight distribution on the mattress makes him wobble as he attempts to lift himself without the use of his arms. April helps to the best of her ability—which is greatly hindered by their laughter.

Somehow, they always end up here.

When Daniel is upright on the edge of the bed with feet on the floor by April's knees, he attempts to escape the 100% cotton handcuffs that have his wrists pinned behind his back. He succeeds, but only in amusing April more.

She reaches her arms around him and pulls his shirt collar up from his ass to his neck. The sleeves follow. Daniel's arms are now covered again by material, but free to move about as he sits in an open shirt on his friend's bed.

April flips his left wrist over and easily slips the cuff button through the cuff button hole. She looks up to find Daniel's face wrinkled in disgust. "Oh, now the fucking thing decides to work."

April laughs again. Daniel leans forward and kisses her smile. It isn't the kind of kiss that says, "Let's get back to the sex." It's impulsive and sweet, and it doesn't ask for anything in return.

It's so benevolent, it stings; like pouring alcohol over a scratch April didn't even realize she had. It's just been so long since she received affection with no motive.

April throws her arms around Daniel's neck. Maybe if she holds him tight enough, she can hold in her emotion. It's been a while, but she's pretty sure crying during sex is still not cool.

Daniel wraps his arms around April's waist. In one gentle swoop, he lies down and pulls her up and over his body so she's back on the right side of the mattress and nestled into him.

April can't wait another minute. She arches her body against Daniel's, moaning softly in his ear as she . . . stretches . . . yawns . . . and falls asleep.

36

Neighborhood Watch

It's New Year's Eve. April tries to finish her errands before businesses close early for the holiday. She makes it to the bank just before noon to deposit her final check from Antic Witties.

As she follows the teller's directions to the bathroom, she passes a long row of empty desks lining the open lobby. The tellers are all working, but the desk bankers have left for the new year. There's only one lonely soul hunched over his computer. April wonders if he has plans for tonight or if, like her, he doesn't know what he wants to do yet.

On her way out of the bathroom, April notices a bowl of butterscotch candies on the lone worker's desk. She hasn't seen butterscotch like this since her grandmother's 1980's candy jar.

"May I have one?" she asks of the balding man.

"Help yourself." He doesn't bother to look up.

It's not until she reaches for the candy that she notices the name plate on the desk.

Arnold Talc

She looks up in surprise to see the legendary coach of the '89 state champs squinting at the computer and talking to himself.

He must feel the stare.

"Can I help you with something?" He looks at April.

"I don't think so," she says. "Thank you for the candy."

"Merry Christmas," he says.

April starts to point out that it's New Year's Eve, but Talc has already turned back to his computer screen.

The instant April steps out of the bank, she wants to text Daniel, but stops herself. Daniel was gone when she woke up this morning. He sent a text saying he had to go into work for end-of-year inventory. Not exactly sexy. Of course, snoring on him last night probably wasn't the pinnacle of sexy either.

She plans to go to The Diner to get lunch for her and Demmy anyway. No, seriously, she would go to The Diner whether it was across the street from where Daniel is working or not.

Maybe she's getting better at lying, because she almost believes that.

As she sits at the counter waiting for her to-go order, April glances casually (or what she hopes is casually) out the window, trying to spot any sign of life at the antique store across the street. The light is on, but she can't see any movement inside. She does a slow, full 360 on her spinning bar stool and notices Evan sitting alone at a booth along the back wall.

He looks up from his phone and also glances casually out the window, but he really looks like it's a sincere casual glance and not a trying-to-be-casual casual glance. When Evan notices April, he smiles and raises his hand in a small wave. She does the same.

With her order in hand, April heads out the front door, glancing at Antic Witties across the way one more time.

At the corner, she says, "Hello, you shiny bastard," to Coach Basham, before taking a left and almost running head first into Alice. Alice Deeds.

"Sorry!" April jumps.

"Who are you talking to?" Alice asks as she looks past April to try to spot another human.

"What?"

"You just called someone a bastard."

"Oh, no. I was just talking to the statue."

"Of course you were."

April feels like that's maybe an insult, like a suggestion that she's the type of person who does weird shit like cuss out statues. But, you know, she was just cussing out a statue so . . .

"Did you have fun last night?" Alice asks this in a way that makes April squirm.

"Yes," April answers, "lots of fun."

These two A-name ladies, acknowledged each other at the wedding, but they never had the chance to speak.

"Good," says Alice with an amused expression. "I heard you made my niece cry."

"Yes. I'm afraid her mom is not a big fan of mine."

"She might like you better than you realize." Alice's tone suggests the mother of the bride got looped in to the makeup scheme.

"I hope so," says April. "I wasn't sure I made the best first impression."

"Yeah, well, you grow on people. Like a . . . zebra mussel."

Alice smiles as if she's joking, so April smiles too (even though she has no idea what a zebra mussel is). Then Alice adds, "You've been good for Mimi."

"She's been good for me," says April.

Alice nods once. "Okay, well, Happy New Year."

"You too," says April. Then she points in the direction of The Diner. "He's waiting for you in there."

Alice's eyebrows narrow. She opens her mouth to protest; to deny she's here to see Evan. But she stops herself and shrugs instead. "Yeah, well, here I am."

Alice heads up the sidewalk toward the shiny bastard.

When Demmy opens her front door, April holds up the food bag. "Have time for a lunch date?"

"Sure," says Demmy as she turns and heads toward her kitchen, "sounds great. And this way, you can talk to me about you and Daniel."

Like Alice did earlier, April opens her mouth to protest, but stops. "We were just dancing. Was it that obvious?" April follows Demmy to the kitchen.

"Yes," says Demmy, "but the kiss on your front lawn was even more obvious."

"Who told you that?!" April feels the unrelenting heat in her cheeks.

"It would be easier for me to tell you who didn't tell me that—the list would be shorter."

"Do people really have nothing better to do?"

"It's called the Neighborhood Watch for a reason," says Demmy.

April groans. No wonder Alice sounded so intentional when she asked if April had fun last night. "It was just a kiss," April lies.

"All night? Because Daniel's car was still in your driveway at 6 a.m. when Samantha York was on her way to work."

"Who's Samantha York?" April asks. "I don't even know her."

"Maiden name is Terry. Her brother is Abe, he was one grade below us. Her mom used to own the stand on 2nd."

"The snow cone lady?" April asks.

"Yes."

"Man, she made the best snow cones."

"She really did," says Demmy.

"So, why is the snow cone lady's daughter gossiping about me?"

"I tried to warn you," says Demmy.

"You did not try to warn me about the snow cone lady's daughter."

Demmy shakes her head. April knows damn well what she means.

April sighs as she sits in a chair at the kitchen table. She unpacks the lunch bag. "If someone said I'm like a zebra muscle, what does that mean? Is it the musculature of a zebra?"

"Different kind of mussel," Demmy says. "It's an invasive species, kind of like a snail, that travels on the bottom of boats from lake to lake and lays a million eggs everywhere it goes."

"That doesn't sound like a compliment," April concludes.

"I don't know," says Demmy. "I guess it depends on how you feel about invaders."

Demmy waits patiently as they eat. April can never leave silence alone for too long. She will eventually say what she came here to say.

After a few bites, April speaks. "I was wondering if I could get the mattress you offered?"

"Sure," says Demmy. "My guys are moving furniture for a staging today. I can ask them to pick it up from storage and bring it by this afternoon."

"It doesn't need to be today," April insists.

"They won't mind," says Demmy. And then she can't help but smile a little. She can read April now. It's nice to have a friend close enough to read. April didn't come here to ask about the mattress. She could call to ask about that. "Next question," says Demmy.

"It's not a question, really," April replies. "I think I'm having a mid-life crisis."

"You think?" says Demmy with one eyebrow raised.

April ignores the sarcasm. "I might really like Daniel. Like, really like him. But this time last year, I thought I was going to be married to Morgan for the rest of my life. Now he's engaged to someone else and having a baby, so, really, what the fuck do I know?" April shrugs.

Demmy sets down her sandwich and looks at her friend. "You know I don't gossip, right? I'm aware of a lot of things I keep to myself because loose lips are bad for business."

"Yes," says April.

"But I'm going to share a secret with you. No one knows anything. We spend our youth thinking we'll figure it out by the time we hit forty. Then we hit forty and don't even know what *IT* is anymore. Everyone our age is questioning everything. Every client over forty who is buying or selling a house is terrified of making a mistake because we have a lot less time to fix what we break."

"Uh, is this supposed to make me feel better?" April asks.

"It's not just you. That's my point. You didn't screw up along the way and end up confused about what you want.

"Married couples our age freak-out wondering if they really want to spend the rest of their life with the jackass they're married to. Single people wonder if they wouldn't be better off married to a jackass than all alone. People with kids worry because their teenagers are ungrateful assholes. People without kids are thinking they missed out on having ungrateful assholes. The people with elderly parents are struggling. The people who lost their parents are struggling.

"We're all realizing we'll never ever be done. There will always be another choice we have to make. Another problem to solve. More work to do. More bills to pay.

"This idea there's only one right answer out there and when we find it, we'll discover joy and peace and rest, is driving us all mad. There is no answer—just more questions."

"That sounds horrible," says April. "I'm actually more hopeless then when I sat down at this table."

"It's not horrible if you can forgive yourself for not having it all figured out."

"But I didn't just think I had it figured out," says April. "I told the world I had it figured out. I made money off of claiming I figured it out."

Demmy stands. "I have to start cooking for the party tonight, but I'm going to give you something a friend gave me when I was going through a hard time, and I want you to promise me you'll look at it."

"Okay," agrees April. "Can I use it as an excuse to get out of the party tonight?"

"You don't have to come tonight," says Demmy as she disappears down her hallway. "There's no right answer."

April raises her voice to be heard over the distance. "I feel like you're using reverse psychology on me."

"No. If I wanted to talk you into coming, I would tell you that Daniel is invited," Demmy shouts from the other room.

"I assumed he was," says April. And that's all she has to say about that.

Demmy reappears with a familiar book in hand. April looks pained as her friend tries to hand her her own damn book.

"No," says April. "Why would I read my own shit?"

"You never know," says Demmy, "you might learn something from your own shit." In response to April's skeptical look, Demmy adds, "At least read the pages I marked. You promised."

April flips through the well-worn copy of her *Great Expectations* to see some passages highlighted with notes in the margins. "You marked this for me?" she asks.

"No," says Demmy. "I marked it for me, years ago, when I needed it."

37

Bureau-Cracy

April sets Demmy's copy of *Great Expectations* on her kitchen counter as though it might detonate. She feels sick at the thought of being reminded how naïve she was when she wrote those words. Demmy asking April to reread her book on successful relationships is like making someone watch a video of the most humiliating moment of their life.

When Demmy convinced April not to burn the original copy of the book, April came home and immediately shoved the book back in the hiding spot on the tall shelf. But now, Demmy's copy of the book sits on April's kitchen counter like a bomb.

She manages to avoid the kitchen for the rest of the afternoon by keeping distracted with fun things like laundry and cleaning out her car. One knows things are bad when one is willing to do chores in order to procrastinate.

Demmy's guys bring the mattress as promised. When they carry it into April's bedroom, one of the guys looks around at the state of things and says, "Just getting moved in?"

"No," says April, "I've been here awhile, actually. I just . . ." but she trails off as they drop the mattress to the ground. She never finishes that statement.

Daniel texts once to "check in". April responds that she's fine. The entire exchange is really a letdown from the height of the previous evening.

April eats cereal for dinner. As she puts the two percent milk away after her meal, she pauses in the cool of the fridge, takes a deep breath, and says to herself, *Fuck it!*

She closes the fridge door and picks up her book (or Demmy's book) from the counter. She leans against the cabinet and lets the book fall open in her hands. It lands on page one-hundred-and-ninety-eight. There's a highlighted passage.

I used to have a book club that met monthly. We'd take turns bringing food. When it was my turn, I brought donuts from a donut shop near where we were meeting. Once I took a bite of one, I lamented that I'd brought very mediocre donuts.

"Why?!" I carried on, "would anyone open a donut shop and sell okay donuts? Wouldn't you want to sell great donuts? I mean, what's the point of trying if you're not trying to be the best?"

"Well," replied a friend, "maybe the point is to be okay."

April remembers the night she added this story to her book. She threw a huge surprise party for Morgan's birthday—his first birthday as a married man. It was a great success. Or, at least, everyone had a great time, especially Morgan. But April realized at the end of the night that she didn't eat any of the food she'd spent all day preparing. She didn't have a glass of the wine from the bottle she picked up from a specialty story in Culver City. She didn't visit with their friends who came in from out of town.

She spent so much time trying to make the party the best it could be, she didn't really get to attend it.

Just before she fell asleep that night, while Morgan was already snoring next to her, she opened her laptop and wrote a chapter for her book. She told the donut story first, then told about the events of the party that night. She can still remember the last line of the chapter . . .

Do I want to be the party planner of my life or do I want to be at the party?

The next morning, April woke up and removed that entire section from her book. She didn't want Morgan to read it and remember his party as the night his wife felt sorry for herself.

But, for whatever reason, just before she sent the final book draft to the editor, April added the donut story back in.

Now, she wonders if the April who wrote the book all those years ago, wrote this message for the April who is reading it now.

What's the point of trying if you're not trying to be the best?

Maybe the point is to be okay.

Great expectations. It's definitely a shitty book title (for anyone other than Charles Dickens) and it may be a shitty way to live a life.

It dawns on April, as she reads her own shit while standing in her own kitchen, she might be slowly pissing on the principal's porch. And long before the divorce, too. Claiming she's not really a writer . . . that's convenient. Because then she doesn't have to try to live up to *Great Expectations*.

Isn't life strange? Success can paralyze you and failure can move you. It can move you halfway across the country and into a different life.

Demmy is right. April isn't stuck. She's done more in the last six months of her life than in the last six years.

Yes, she failed to live up to the big dreams she had for her life. But maybe those big dreams have failed her, too.

April looks at the faded coral wall behind her kitchen table made of boxes. All those years she spent lost in building the perfect house for her and Morgan.

All those years she waited for a great romance. All those years trying to make her life live up to a best-selling story. Years of living in the shadows of big dreams. Waiting, chasing, sacrificing, because it would be worth it when she had the big love and the big life she was waiting for. A lifetime of waiting to live.

She could never catch the moon.

If April's life, if the goal is to be okay, then . . . volunteering in the community would be meaningful. Making a friend happy on her wedding would matter. Wrapping gifts with a nice little bow would be a sweet way to bring more beauty into the world.

And going to a party to hang out with a guy she has a crush on would be a pleasant way to spend New Year's Eve.

April closes her book.

She blasts music at full volume on her phone, as she scrambles out of sweatpants and into jeans. Her hair gets pulled up and her lips get glossed.

She puts her phone in her purse, still blaring music as she throws open her front door . . . and screams.

So does Daniel.

They both stand with their hands on their pounding hearts, trying to regain some composure.

"I'm so sorry," Daniel yells over the music. "I was just about to knock."

It takes April a couple of attempts to dig her phone out of the purse and get the music turned off. "No, it's okay. I just was not expecting a man on the other side of this door."

"Were you expecting a woman?" Daniel asks.

"No," says April, "I was expecting no one. I was going to head to the party."

"Want a chauffeur?"

"Sure. Yes. That'd be great."

Daniel steps aside to allow April to exit her house and lock her front door. She asks about the wine bottle in his hand. "Is that for the party?"

"It certainly can be."

"Well," says April, "I didn't bring anything, so now I'll look like less of an asshole."

"Hey, happy I can help." The truck headlights pop on when Daniel unlocks the doors with the key fob. He opens the passenger door for April and hands her the wine bottle.

As Daniel walks around the front of the truck to the driver's side, April sees him in the headlights, looking very cute in his vintage Spice Girls concert t-shirt and jeans. It makes her heart skip a little. Daniel climbs in the driver's side with a smile. They pull away from April's house.

"Guess who I saw today," April says.

"Demmy," Daniel answers.

"No," says April. "Well, yes. But no. I saw Arnold Talc."

"How was he?"

"He was . . . a week behind."

"What does that mean?" Daniel stops at the intersection at the end of the block.

"I don't really want to go to the party," April answers.

Daniel looks at her to see if she's joking. She's not.

"Great," he says as he puts the truck in park. "Because I actually came to your house to ask you if I could please come in."

"Sounds familiar," April smiles.

"And have a glass of wine from the bottle you're holding."

"Okay."

"And maybe go up to your bedroom."

"I'm listening."

"And . . . with your consent, of course . . . "

"Mmmhmmm."

"I would like to put together that bureau that's been sitting there for months."

April laughs. "That does not sound like a fun New Year's Eve for you."

"It does," says Daniel, "because you'll be there."

This makes April feel something that feels a lot like joy. It might be joy. Even though it scares her, April says, "The only reason I was going to the party was because I was hoping to see you there."

"Well, here I am." Daniel puts the car in reverse and brings his hand to the back of April's headrest. He leans closer to her than he has to as he twists to see out his rear window. He backs up all the way down her street.

"We really can do something more fun than putting together my furniture." April watches everything around her fly by in reverse.

"You don't understand," says Daniel, "that bureau has haunted me ever since I first brought it up to your room. I don't like to leave furniture in boxes - too much wasted potential."

April looks out the truck to the upstairs window of her house. She imagines Daniel's shadow there.

"Besides," Daniel adds as he finishes parking the truck, "I'll take any excuse to be in your bedroom."

April looks at him. "I got an actual mattress today."

"Really?!"

"Don't get too excited. It's still on the floor. I don't even have a bed frame."

"Baby steps," says Daniel. He lays his hand on the middle console, palm up,

210

as an offering. April puts her hand on his and their fingers mix.

"What happened to just being friends?" she asks.

"That was a dumb idea," Daniel says. "I knew it was dumb as soon as you suggested it at the coffee shop that day."

"It was the elf costume that changed your mind, wasn't it?"

"You're joking, but I really like that elf costume."

"We could still hurt each other, you know," she says.

"Oh, I know," he says, as he gives her hand a squeeze. "Are you sure you're ready for this? I don't mean to push you into having an actual functional bureau if you're not ready for it."

April considers this for a moment.

"I think I'll be okay," she says.

Daniel leans forward to kiss her before abruptly letting go of her hand and opening his car door. "Alright," he says as he steps out of the truck, "but I do have to warn you, building things is my foreplay."

April's laughter fills the truck.

And for the first time in a long time, she doesn't want to be anywhere but where she is right now—with Daniel coming to open her door.

About the Author

I live in Texas with my favorite husband and my favorite kids. (They are also my only husband and kids, if you're concerned about that.)

I've had a lot of creative careers in my life, but writing has been my home since childhood. It's the way I get back to myself.

A few years ago, a cancer diagnosis and the subsequent treatments changed the trajectory of my life dramatically. I absolutely did not want to write a book about cancer (and I beg other writers to please find another "something tragic happens plot point" because I don't want to read any more about cancer). But I did want to write about a woman my age who finds her life on a very different path than she imagined.

I wanted to write a romance because romance novels are my favorite escape. And I wanted to write a romance about a good guy (like my husband is) because good guys can be sexy as hell and it's time to celebrate them.

I actually do believe in great love stories. I just don't believe they have to be filled with flowers and jewelry and other grand gestures. I think great love stories are about two people sharing the work of life—the small, daily tasks we do just so that our partner doesn't have to.

Great love is about washing the dishes.